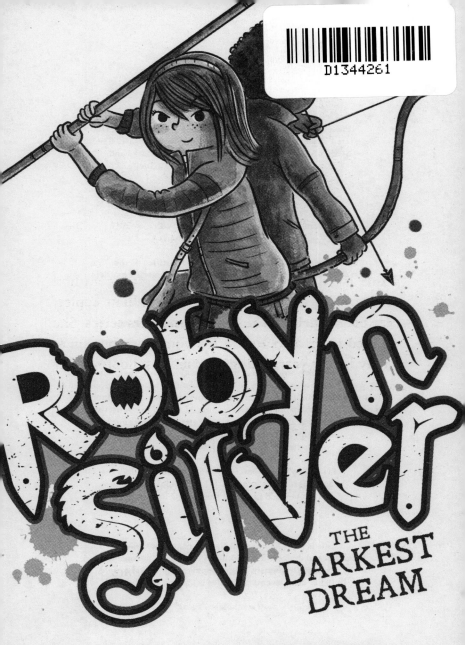

ROBYN SILVER

THE DARKEST DREAM

PAULA HARRISON

■SCHOLASTIC

Scholastic Children's Books
An imprint of Scholastic Ltd
Euston House, 24 Eversholt Street, London, NW1 1DB, UK
Registered office: Westfield Road, Southam, Warwickshire, CV47 0RA
SCHOLASTIC and associated logos are trademarks and/or
registered trademarks of Scholastic Inc.

First published in the UK by Scholastic Ltd, 2017

Text copyright © Paula Harrison, 2017
Illustration copyright © Dave Kurtz Williams, 2017
- in the style of Renée Kurilla

The right of Paula Harrison to be identified as the
author and illustrator of this work has been asserted by them.

ISBN 978 1407 17059 6

Printed by CPI Group (UK) Ltd, Croydon, CR0 4YY
Papers used by Scholastic Children's Books are made
from wood grown in sustainable forests.

1 3 5 7 9 10 8 6 4 2

www.scholastic.co.uk

For James

Monster Mayhem Ruins Our Picnic

I bet lots of people think being a monster-hunter is really awesome. Some parts are cool, I suppose, like practising new sword moves in the garden at Grimdean House. But if you think I spend the whole time defeating monsters so that everyone can tell me how grateful they are, you're dead wrong.

For a start, most people can't see monsters. Only people like me, Aiden and Nora can, because we're Chimes – born on the stroke of midnight. This means our monster-hunting has to be completely secret so that ordinary people don't get freaked out. Monsters can still hurt you though, whether you can see them or not. That's why Mr Cryptorum says we have a sacred duty to protect everyone in

Wendleton, because we're the only ones who can fight the grodders, the bogguns, the scree sags and all the other horrible creatures out there.

Cryptorum goes on about it quite a lot – tells us that now we're Chimes we must always put our monster-fighting duties first. It's always the same speech so I tend to stop listening and think about what might be for dinner instead. Cryptorum is the one that trains us – teaches us how to fight and where each monster's weak spots are. He's been a Chime for a gazillion years so he knows a lot.

It's easy for him though. All he has to do is sit in his huge mansion, read the dusty old books in his study and polish the monster-fighting weapons he keeps in his shed. He doesn't have schoolwork like I do or four brothers and sisters who steal my pizza, hog the TV and basically drive me mad.

What happened one Saturday reminded me just how impossible it is trying to be a Chime with my family around. It was the first sunny weekend in ages and Mum had decided we'd go on a family picnic. I love picnics – especially if there's lots of cake – but what if Mum chose somewhere infested with monsters like Blagdurn Heath? It's bad enough getting rid of the ants and wasps crawling round the picnic basket without fighting off spiny kobolds and huge hairy grodders as well.

I patted the jeans pocket that held my torchblade. It was a torch with a hidden silver blade inside which Aiden had invented. No one looking at it would guess it was more than a torch, which meant our mission to fight monsters could stay secret. It was so handy that I kept it in my pocket all the time these days. "Maybe we could just have the picnic in the garden?" I suggested, thinking that would be safer.

My older sister, Sammie, who was making these really soggy-looking cheese sandwiches, stopped buttering bread to roll her eyes and sigh deeply. Sammie and I don't get on that well which is basically because she's a great big pain.

"You want to have it in the garden?" Mum piled apples and oranges into the picnic basket. "That's not very exciting! Where's your sense of adventure, Robyn? You used to like Blagdurn Heath."

"Yeah," I muttered under my breath. "That was before I fought an army of monsters there and nearly fell off a cliff."

It was true. There'd been a massive battle on the heath right before Christmas and Aiden, Nora and me had been surrounded by masses of monsters. I still got a funny hollow feeling in my stomach when I remembered it.

"What's that?" Mum asked.

"Oh, nothing!" I said quickly. "Have we got any cake to take with us?"

Mum took a square container out of the cupboard. Inside was a large chocolate cake covered with chocolaty icing and sprinkles. "Ta-da! I didn't have time to make it myself but never mind."

Annie, my younger sister, ran straight in as if the cake was a magnet. "Yummy! Can I have a slice now?"

Mum clapped the lid on the container. "No, you have to wait till we get there! Now hurry up and find your shoes."

Dad came in, whistling. My brothers, Ben and Josh, were in the hallway scuffling over a football. Ben, who was sixteen and twice Josh's size, was winning easily.

"I think we should *definitely* go to Blagdurn Heath." Sammie packed up the sandwiches in paper bags. "I love it up there."

I ignored her. She was only saying that because she knew I didn't want to go.

"We could go to Penhurst Park," Dad said. "It'll only take ten minutes to walk there. Has anyone seen my keys? I'm sure I left them on the hall table."

I screwed my eyes up, thinking hard. What was the chance of meeting a monster in Penhurst Park? It was just a park with a playground at one end. No woods for kobolds to hide in. No dark corners for lurking scree sags. Surely we'd be safe there.

It took us nearly an hour to get to Penhurst Park, mainly because Annie needed a wee when we were halfway down the road and we had to go all the way back home again. Annie's only six and she's the baby of the family so she gets spoilt by everyone. Ben is the eldest – he's sixteen. Then Sammie's fourteen, I'm eleven and Josh is eight.

I'm the third out of us five Silver kids, stuck right in the middle. Half the time Mum and Dad tell me to be more responsible and the rest of the time they say I'm not old enough to make grown-up decisions. If they knew it was my duty to protect the town from dangerous monsters they'd probably say Wendleton was doomed and book us all on a plane to Alaska.

On the way to the park, we passed Ashbrook Street where I used to go to school. Three huge trees had fallen on the school roof one night last autumn. They'd done so much damage that the whole roof had collapsed and repair work had been going on for ages. The school had moved into Grimdean House, owned by Mr Cryptorum, with its dungeon full of monsters and a shed full of bats in the garden.

Even from the end of the street I could see the top of an orange crane, stretching over our old playground like a mechanical giraffe. Obviously the building work was still far from finished.

"Hurry up!" Mum rushed us down the road and round the corner. "Here's a good place." Reaching the wide stretch of grass near the playground, Mum laid out the first picnic rug.

We take three rugs every time we have a picnic because there are so many of us and because Annie always insists on having one rug all to herself.

"Can we eat?" Ben already had the picnic basket open.

There was a whirl of arms as me, Sammie, Josh and Annie all dived for the food at the same time.

Mum snatched the cake container away before we could get to it. "Honestly! Does it have to be like feeding time at the zoo? We'll save the cake till later – to eat after we've played some games."

We all sat and munched happily for a while and then Mum took Annie to the playground, while Sammie, Ben and Josh started a game of rounders and Dad lay down on the rug and shut his eyes.

After a few minutes, Dad's breathing slowed and three silvery moths blinked into the air and fluttered round his head. I watched them for a minute. Dream moths were beautiful and it gave me a jolt of excitement knowing I was the only one who would be able to see them. I loved the way they dipped and danced around the person sleeping. I wasn't sure where they came from, but they reminded me that not all the things I saw these days were monsters. I could see dreams and I could even see wishes just because I'd been born on the stroke of midnight.

I finished my sandwich and got up to join in with the rounders, leaving Dad snoozing on the rug, but as I crossed the grass I saw strange ripples twisting at the centre of the boating lake. I crept towards the trees that surrounded the lake. The disturbance in the water was a real whirlpool and it was growing – as if something was sucking the water from below. Luckily no one else seemed to have noticed it – probably because the trees around the lake blocked their view. People were playing football and eating ice cream as if everything was normal.

Was the whirlpool created by currents in the water or was it made by the wind? I sighed. There was no chance I'd be that lucky.

The tip of a white tentacle lifted lazily out of the water and then vanished again. Panic squeezed my stomach. Why hadn't I thought of the lake when Dad suggested coming here? Why hadn't I thought of water monsters?

I glanced round. Mum and Annie were still at the playground and the others were busy with their rounders game. I just had to sneak away.

Dad opened his eyes and the dream moths vanished. "Aren't you going to play rounders, Robyn?" he called over to me.

I stopped, feeling caught, and my gaze fell on the soggy cheese sandwiches. They were the only things left to eat, apart from the chocolate cake, which Mum had hidden somewhere. I ran back and grabbed them, ignoring the disgusting smell. "I'll play rounders later. I'm going to feed the ducks first."

"Aren't you a bit old for feeding ducks?" said Dad, but I pretended I didn't hear him.

I tucked the cheese sandwiches into my coat pocket and slipped through the trees. I couldn't take my eyes off the churning vortex in the middle of the lake. There was still no one else near the water. It was lucky no one had decided to take a rowing boat out for a spin.

I ran on to the wooden jetty where the boats were tied up and peered into the murky water. A huge jelly-like mass floated below the surface and its six eyes narrowed suspiciously as it spotted me.

It was a nesha – the biggest, deadliest water monster in the Unseen World.

I shuddered. If some little kid decided they wanted to go out in a boat it would be the last thing they ever did. What should I do – jump into the water and fight, or try to lure it out of the lake?

The nesha decided for me. It lunged out of the water, its tentacles writhing. I leapt back but one tentacle fastened on to my coat, gripping my sleeve with its sucker. I yanked the torchblade from my pocket and jabbed frantically at the button. The torch casing opened and the silver blade sprang up.

I swung my arm, slashing the tentacle holding on to me – a classic sideswipe move that Cryptorum had taught me. The blade sliced through the slimy sucker. The tentacle recoiled and the broken end thudded on to the wooden jetty, still wriggling.

The other tentacles writhed and a deep roar made the whole lake tremble. Then a spout of water erupted, drenching me completely. I pushed my dripping hair out of my eyes. "Is that the worst you can do?" I snapped, forgetting that was the sort of thing you should NEVER say to a monster.

Two thick tentacles coiled round my waist, gripping me tight and lifting me into the air.

"Robyn, where are you?" Mum called from the other side of the trees.

"Um . . . just a minute!" I gasped, as the tentacles swung me over the water. I could see Mum and Annie making their way back from the playground.

The nesha swung me upside down and whirled me round and round. A gurgling noise came from below the surface as if the monster was laughing at me. My right arm was pinned so I passed the torchblade to my left and drove it into the nearest tentacle.

Roaring, the nesha dropped me on the jetty. The sword fell out of my hand and I stumbled to my knees. Before I could get my breath back, the nesha propelled itself right out of the lake. Its jaws opened like a cavern bristling with giant, razor-sharp teeth.

My heart thumped against my ribs. The torchblade lay gleaming on the wooden boards. It was too far away. I'd never reach it. The nesha emerged from the water in horrible slow motion.

Panicking, I used the only thing I had. Pulling the cheese sandwiches out of my pocket, I chucked them at the nesha's colossal gaping mouth. They bounced off its teeth and rolled down its purple, blister-spotted tongue. For a second, the monster looked confused. Then a deep gurgling noise came from the back of its throat.

There was a horrible pause. Then with one huge belch, the cheese sandwiches came flying out of its mouth with such force they landed right at the top of a nearby tree. The smell of half-digested cheese wafted over the water.

The monster glared at me as if wondering whether I had anything even more disgusting in my pockets. Then it sank below the surface. Who knew Sammie's vile sandwiches would be so handy?

The chopped-off end of a tentacle was still wriggling – trying to worm its way along the jetty – so I kicked it into the water. Maybe chopped-off nesha tentacles could rejoin the monster's body. I'd have to ask Nora. She would know.

I glanced round quickly. The lake was screened

by trees and luckily no one was close enough to see what had happened. I'd have to go to Grimdean House and tell Cryptorum there was a nesha in the park that needed sorting out. For now, I'd probably done enough to make sure the creature would stay hidden under the water.

I picked up my silver blade and pushed the button so that the sword slotted down inside the torch again. Then I grabbed a big signpost that read CLOSED and stood it at the entrance to the jetty. That should stop people from going boating for now.

Through the trees I could just about see my family sitting on the picnic rugs. They must have finished the rounders game without me. I glanced down at my sodden jeans and T-shirt. I was going to have to think of a reason why I was soaked. A monster-sized duck maybe?

I slipped back through the trees. Mum and Dad were sitting on one picnic rug and Sammie and Ben had the second one. Josh was kicking the rounders ball against a tree. Annie was lying across the third rug in a starfish shape, a pile of daisies beside her.

"Did you find any ducks, Robyn?" Mum twisted round to look at me. "What on earth have you been doing?"

I scraped my wet fringe off my face. "It was just an accident," I muttered.

"You fell in, didn't you?" Sammie's eyes lit up. "Another Robyn disaster!"

This was a family joke – that I was a bit of a disaster area. I didn't get into that many scrapes.

"Maybe she went in on purpose for a swim," Ben joked.

"Look, you're dripping all over the place!" Mum sighed. "Don't sit down here. You'll make the rug all wet. Honestly! I can't take you lot anywhere."

"I didn't do anything!" Annie piped up. "I wouldn't fall in the water like Robyn did."

"I didn't fall in, exactly," I said, stung.

"Can I go in the lake?" Josh asked.

"NO!" Mum and Dad said in unison.

"Don't worry – I'm nearly dry." I shook water off my sleeve. I needed to change the subject. "So can we have the chocolate cake now?"

There was a pause and Sammie smirked.

Then I noticed the empty plates lying on the grass scattered with dark brown crumbs. "Hey! Did you eat it already?"

Mum lifted up the empty cake box and peered inside. "I thought someone had saved you a piece.

Sorry, Robyn. I did call you but you took a while to come back."

"You ate the cake without me?" I huffed. "Well thanks!" Why was I so surprised? That was the main rule in our family: if you wanted to eat you had to fight for it. Nothing tasty lasted for very long.

"Never mind. You'll get some cake another day," Dad said heartily. "Now who's for another game of rounders?"

They all started arguing over who was to bat and who was to field. I sighed and rummaged inside the picnic basket to see if there was an apple or an orange left. It wasn't that I expected a round of applause for dealing with the lake monster but a slice of chocolate cake would have been nice.

The torchblade fell out of my pocket and rolled across the grass. I froze as Sammie picked it up. It would have to be her.

"What's this?" She turned it over in her hands.

"What does it look like?" I said.

Sammie eyed me scornfully. Then she chucked the torchblade at me and I caught it. "You're weird, Robyn. What did you bring a torch to a picnic for?" She turned away before I could answer.

Pushing the torchblade deep into my pocket, I

breathed out slowly. That had been close. If she'd pressed the right button, the silver blade – so deadly to monsters – would have appeared right in front of everyone. I had to make sure she never got hold of the torchblade again. How could my family understand that I needed to carry a sword when they couldn't see the things I had to fight? They must never find out about me being a Chime.

"Robyn?" Annie clutched my hand. "Can you come and push me on the swing?"

"Sure!" I glanced at the lake again but the water was still. Hopefully that nesha wouldn't resurface for a really long time.

Mr Cryptorum Gets
His Orders

couldn't stop picturing the nesha when I was sitting in class the following afternoon. It was definitely the biggest monster I'd ever fought and its bulging eyes had looked so angry. I could still feel its slimy tentacles on my skin...

"Robyn Silver! Where's the rest of your work?" Mrs Perez, our class teacher, was standing over me, her eyes fixed on my history book like a searchlight.

"Um..." I gazed down at the half a sentence I'd written. Had I been daydreaming all this time?

"Well? Where's the rest of your work?" Mrs Perez repeated.

A few kids sniggered behind me and the teacher

silenced them with a look. Sometimes I thought I'd rather face a monster than Mrs Perez in a cross mood. Luckily the bell went for the end of the day and I was saved.

"Take this work home and bring it to me first thing tomorrow," she told me crisply, before clapping her hands for quiet.

As soon as we were dismissed, I pushed my way through the crowded corridor and headed upstairs past rooms full of antique furniture and old paintings to Cryptorum's study on the top floor of Grimdean House. This was where we always met for Bat Club, which was our cover story for Chime training. Everyone thought it was a wildlife club we went to after school. Well, we couldn't exactly tell them we were learning to fight ettings and bogguns.

Cryptorum's assistant, Miss Smiting (who was half woman and half snake), was the one who'd thought of calling it Bat Club. It was named after the bats that lived in the huge barn in the Grimdean garden (bats that were actually kept for tracking monsters). The club was a good cover, but it meant we sometimes had to pretend to learn stuff and make nesting boxes and bird feeders, which was a massive waste of time when we could have been practising sword moves.

The noise of kids leaving their classrooms drifted up the stairs. Grimdean House belonged to Mr Cryptorum and it had been the only place big enough to take in our whole school when the three trees had collapsed on the school roof last autumn. It was a huge grey mansion with hundreds of rooms full of glass cabinets, grand pianos and paintings of Cryptorum's ancestors. There were secret passages inside the walls that led down to the dungeon where Cryptorum kept the captured monsters until he decided what to do with them. Mirrors hung on every wall. They were great for trapping phantom-like monsters such as bogguns who obviously liked their own reflections way too much.

On the pointed tower was a huge golden clock that often made my skin prickle when it chimed. It was called a Mortal Clock and it had awoken our Chime powers when it struck midnight many months ago. I didn't really understand why it had worked that way. Nora said the very first Chimes had developed the skill of clock-making to pass their abilities on – she'd read all about it in Cryptorum's history books. I liked the books describing sword moves better.

Anyway, having lessons in a creepy old mansion filled with bats, dungeons and secret passages had started to feel pretty normal now. Last term, I found out the damage to our old school roof had been arranged by Miss Smiting, who had been searching for new Chimes to help Mr Cryptorum in the never-ending battle against the monsters. Cryptorum was becoming old and creaky, although he got really grouchy with anyone who pointed that out.

I bounced into the study and Nora, who'd got there before me, cast me a warning look.

Cryptorum looked up from the note about the nesha that I'd left on his desk this morning. "What on earth was a nesha doing in Penhurst Park? Those monsters are never seen in town – ever!" He glared round so fiercely that Nora scurried behind an armchair. Then he waved the note at me and his eyebrows rose alarmingly. "Well? Why was the nesha there?"

"Sorry, I forgot to ask it! Perhaps it came for an ice cream." I knew joking around would annoy Cryptorum but I couldn't help myself. "Maybe slime flavour!"

Cryptorum scowled at me. Underneath his bristling eyebrows, he had deep brown eyes and a craggy nose. His grey hair, which got wilder when he was cross, looked like an evil pixie had attacked him with a hairdryer. "This is not a joke, young lady. Neshas are the deadliest water monsters of the Unseen World. They're exceptionally strong and have a very bad temper!"

"You're telling me!" I muttered, rubbing my arm. I was definitely going to have bruises where that beast had grabbed me.

"I just don't understand it!" Cryptorum said. "Neshas don't like being around people. They like swamps in the middle of nowhere."

"Um … well actually, *The Compendium of Ancient Beasts and Fiends* tells of a water monster that was seen in the River Thames in 1646." Nora's freckled face lit up as she remembered what she'd read. "That was right in the middle of London. . ." She broke off as Cryptorum shot her a grumpy look.

"Maybe the monster just got confused about where it was," I suggested.

Cryptorum snorted and resumed pacing up and down. I went over to the window and gazed out. Cryptorum's stomping would probably go on for ages. I didn't see why he was in such a bad mood about the monster. He wasn't the one who'd missed out on chocolate cake.

Down below, Obediah Brown – the Grimdean

gardener – was raking dead leaves away from the spring flowers. One bat flapped lazily over the roof of the barn where a hundred more of its kind would be sleeping. There was no breeze and that made it a perfect day for archery practice. I hoped Aiden would hurry up and get here so that we could start. We were a team – Aiden and Nora and me. We'd all been born on the stroke of midnight and we'd all found out that we were Chimes together here at Grimdean House last autumn when Miss Smiting had taken us down to the dungeon to look at the monsters of the Unseen World for the very first time. It was weird to think that had only been five months ago.

The door swung open and Miss Smiting glided in. Her long skirt swept along the floor, hiding what I'd always suspected was a snake-like lower half. Her bright green eyes with slit-like pupils read our expressions in a moment. "Why the glum facess?" she hissed. "Is there bad newss?"

"A nesha at Penhurst Park," Cryptorum told her and explained what I'd seen.

I glanced back at the garden. Where was Aiden? He'd never missed Bat Club before without saying something. The clock on the tower began to chime.

"Right! I'm going to search the park." Cryptorum

shrugged on a coat but before he could reach the door someone knocked firmly.

"Who'ss there?" called Miss Smiting.

"Those teachers are supposed to stay downstairs," Cryptorum muttered. "I always said we shouldn't let them hold their school here, Junella."

"I will deal with it." Miss Smiting swung the door open. "Can I help you?"

A man in a long coat holding a black briefcase towered over her. His thin lips flexed into an even thinner smile. "Good afternoon. I'm Mr Thomas Fettle and I'm here to see Erasmus Cryptorum. A lady downstairs told me to come straight up." His eyes flicked round the room very fast, lingering on me and Nora for a second. "I'm from the International Federation of Chimes."

"Well you can go straight back there!" Cryptorum growled. "I told the last messenger who came here twenty years ago – I don't need any help. I'm getting on just fine by myself."

I nudged Nora. We'd both known there was a Chime organisation somewhere in the world but we'd never met anyone from it before. I'd thought the man would be wilder, with a long beard and a dagger between his teeth maybe. This guy looked so boring and normal.

"*You* may be fine but it's not just about you any more, is it?" Mr Fettle's eyes fixed on me and Nora again, as if he was measuring how good or bad we were. His stare gave me a horrible wriggly feeling in the pit of my stomach. "What are your names, children?"

I stiffened. I hated being called *children* like that. "I'm Robyn Silver."

"I'm Nora Juniper," Nora squeaked.

"And where's the third one – the boy?" Mr Fettle asked.

Cryptorum's eyebrows bristled like poisonous caterpillars looking for a fight. "How do you know about the kids I'm training? Who talked to you?"

"I am not at liberty to reveal that but I should remind you that the Federation prides itself on being well informed," Mr Fettle said stiffly. "Before we go any further I must check the most important matter: is the heart of your clock still functioning?"

"Yes, it's functioning," Cryptorum said through gritted teeth.

Nora and me exchanged puzzled glances. What did he mean *the heart of the clock*? Was that some sort of code?

Striding past Miss Smiting and Cryptorum,

Mr Fettle set his briefcase down on Cryptorum's desk and pressed the catch to let the lid swing open. Inside was a neat array of pencils, pens and rulers, a square lunchbox and a scroll of paper fastened with a black band. Eye, the crab-like monster Cryptorum kept as a pet, crept out of a desk drawer and sidled up to the case for a closer look.

Mr Fettle snatched up a ruler as if to swat her, but I shot forwards and put my arm in the way. "Don't touch her!" I snapped. "She's very shy."

"I had no intention of hurting her." Fettle set down the ruler and Eye scuttled behind the briefcase. I didn't believe him. He'd certainly looked like he was about to do something. I folded my arms, watching him closely.

Picking up the scroll, Fettle removed the band and let the paper unfurl till it dangled to the floor. The scroll was covered with black squiggly writing, as if ants had walked through ink and then run all around the page.

"Get on with it then!" Cryptorum said irritably. "What is it this time? A declaration on the meanness of scree sags? Fifty guidelines for spotting a boggun? If only the Federation would get off their backsides and do some actual fighting, we wouldn't have to be tortured with their endless announcements."

Mr Fettle sucked his breath in sharply. "These are not announcements. They are *orders*. And may I remind you that you answer to the Federation as every Chime does and you would do well to pay attention."

Cryptorum looked as if he was about to launch himself at the other man. Miss Smiting put a hand on his shoulder to hold him back.

Fettle cleared his throat and began reading. "*At 12:53 on Wednesday 9th March, the Grand Master of the Clocks measured a spike in dark energy readings. This matched a similar but smaller spike last December, and after many calculations he believes that a monster of significant power is about to rise here in Wendleton.*" He paused for effect and Cryptorum made a scornful snort.

"I've heard about the Grand Master of the Clocks," Nora whispered to me. "There's a whole circle of Mortal Clocks at Chime headquarters and the Grand Master sits in the centre attached to the clocks with wires and a metal plate strapped to his head. He can monitor the whole world and find out which places have the most monsters by being connected to the clocks."

"Sounds weird!" I murmured back. "Why would you want to be attached to clocks with wires? What if your brain got fried?"

Mr Fettle shot us a cold look. "On a more personal note, I've spent the last three days investigating the area, and the scale of monster activity here is deeply disturbing. I tracked two scree sags to an alley and found a grodder in a supermarket car park. History tells us that every time something big rises there is an escalation of monster activity leading up to it. I can only assume that you have not been paying close enough attention to what's going on round here."

"Rubbish! You find a couple of scree sags and you think you know everything about this town." Cryptorum lifted his eyebrows scornfully but I knew he must be thinking about the nesha – a monster that had never come into Wendleton before. There had been more monster activity round here lately and he knew it.

Mr Fettle ignored Cryptorum's comment and continued reading from the scroll. "*Therefore the Grand Master of the Clocks has decreed that all Chimes living in a thirty mile radius of this town shall prepare to fight this new threat whatever it may be. In addition, all adults who are training young Chime children shall make sure their trainees are ready to fight. They must obey the following orders and if they fail to do so they will be expelled from the Federation. Order number one: three hours of weapons training must be done every day. Order number two. . ."*

I brightened up. Weapons training – now he was talking!

". . . frostblades shall be made from Prague silver and no swords made from other metals will be acceptable. Order number three: all members shall provide weekly reports on the young Chimes' progress along with evidence that they are being trained properly. Order number four. . ."

I scuffed the carpet with my toe. This was turning into a LOT of orders. I was never going to remember them all. Would mum have started cooking dinner yet? Please please let it be pizza for tea.

". . . Order number twenty-three. Chimes will not leave the area without informing the Federation. . ."

Fettle's voice droned on and the list of orders seemed endless. I stifled a yawn. I daydreamed that I was back at the park, fighting the nesha. This time I dodged before the monster could catch me in its tentacles and with a swing of my sword I sent it howling to the bottom of the lake. Somehow, in my daydream, I ended up slicing the chocolate cake neatly with my torchblade and my family applauded and offered me the first three slices. Yeah, like that would ever happen.

"I SHALL NOT BE ORDERED ABOUT LIKE A SCHOOLBOY!" Cryptorum roared.

I jumped. So did Fettle, though he tried to hide it. His finger slipped from where it had been pointing at order number eighty-seven, which read, *Trainees shall be given a Chime wolf by the Federation to help them track monsters.*

"The International Federation of Chimes will not allow you to train these children if you do not follow orders," Fettle told Cryptorum. "So you have no choice."

"We'll see about that! I'm phoning the Grand Master right now." Cryptorum marched out of the room.

Just after Cryptorum stormed out, Aiden came in carrying a long wooden frame with a metal lever in the middle. "Sorry I'm late. I was just finishing off this slingshot. It'll shoot arrows much further than a bow and now I just need to make it stronger. . ." He tailed off, staring at Fettle.

"This is Mr Fettle from the International Federation of Chimes," I told him.

Fettle pursed his thin lips. "This is worse than I thought. . . You're making unauthorized weapons here." He jabbed a bony finger at Aiden's invention. "That device is not within Federation rules!"

Aiden's face fell.

"Then your rules are wrong!" I said.

Rolling up the scroll, Fettle put it beside his sandwich box before snapping the briefcase shut. He picked up the case and faced Miss Smiting. "There are too many irregularities going on here. I'm afraid I shall have to make a full report to the Federation."

Miss Smiting's eyes blazed as she advanced on Fettle and the hissing in her voice grew more menacing. "Don't forget to include a description of the ssnake woman running the place. I hear she bitess!"

Looking alarmed, Fettle hurried to the door.

"Hey, what about the next order you were going to read? What about the Chime wolf you're supposed to give us?" I called.

"I'm sorry – the last available Chime wolf was given to the children I visited before you." Fettle dashed to the stairs. "And having seen you all, I doubt you're responsible enough to train a wolf anyway."

"We ARE responsible!" I said. "We even fed the bats once." But Mr Fettle was gone. Miss Smiting swept out after him.

"What's going on?" Aiden put down the slingshot and brushed sawdust off his hands. "That guy didn't seem very happy."

Nora told him about the surge in dark energy that the Federation had measured and how it was supposed to mean that a really dangerous monster would appear. "The spike in dark energy's happened before – I've read about it. Every time it occurs a really nasty beast turns up, but it's a different one each time so no one knows what it'll look like or how to kill it. The last time this happened was eleven years ago, when a gigantic sea wurm appeared and swallowed an island off the coast of Norway."

"So we have no idea which monster it'll be," I said, once Nora had finished. "All we know is that we're basically doomed."

"Hold on a minute – why were you talking about a wolf just now?" Aiden asked me.

"That was the next thing the Federation man was going to read off his scroll – we're supposed to be given a wolf to help us track down monsters," I said.

"Looking after a wolf sounds dangerous!" Nora shuddered.

"Sounds more fun than hunting with those flappy old bats that Cryptorum keeps in the garden. Maybe they'll find an extra wolf for us," I said hopefully.

Having a wolf for a pet sounded perfect to me.

We Run into Something Worse Than a Nesha

Aiden, Nora and me spent the rest of the afternoon practising sword skills on the Grimdean lawn. We didn't see Cryptorum till the following day when he marched down the garden at twilight. "Bring your weapons," he said. "The nesha's moved out of the park and I've tracked it to the edge of town. It must be using the town drains to get around." He flung open the weapons shed, revealing rows of gleaming silver frostblades hanging on the wall along with several racks of bows and arrows.

I caught a glimpse of Cryptorum's best sword – a gleaming silver blade with swirly markings that looked like an alphabet from ancient times.

"Can I borrow that sword? I promise I'll look after it."

"No, you can't!" Cryptorum snapped. "It's hundreds of years old and much too valuable for the likes of you."

I stuck my torchblade in my pocket and chose a bow and some arrows. I'd borrowed the sword with the swirly markings to fight monsters on Blagdurn Heath before Christmas and I'd found it so light and easy to handle. I was desperate to try it out again but I guess Cryptorum hadn't really forgiven me for taking it without asking.

Five minutes later, I was sitting between Nora and Aiden on the back seat of Cryptorum's shiny black limousine as Miss Smiting swung us round every bend in Wendleton at top speed. Screeching into a car park, she slammed on the brakes. "Here we are – good luck, Chimes!"

I climbed out and zipped on the tough leather jacket which was the closest thing we had to armour. Water glistened behind a clump of trees. "This is Foxtail Brook," I said. "We came here once for a picnic on Ben's birthday."

"The bats flew over earlier and located the nesha," Cryptorum told us. "With any luck it'll still be here – look for tentacles below the water."

I walked up to the riverbank and pointed my torch at the dark water. "I can't see anything!"

Aiden joined me. "Maybe I should invent a torchblade with a stronger light. I bet I could do it if I made the casing longer."

Aiden was always working on new ideas. Last week, he'd invented a tracker spray for the bats so we'd know exactly where they were all the time, especially when they were hunting down monsters. It was unlucky that the spray had sent the bats wild. They'd dive-bombed the local chip shop, causing panic and making people spill chips everywhere. Cryptorum had banned him from using it after that.

"What we really need for this job is a tentacle detector," I said, eyeing the water. "Something that beeps before the sucker reaches out of the water and grabs you!"

"Shh!" Nora said in a strangled whisper. "I was reading *Unseen Creatures of the Lake and Swamp* the other day and it said neshas have better hearing than bats. They can hear sounds from miles away AND the suction pad on each tentacle is stronger than ten men."

A cold prickle ran down my neck. At least with Nora's information we always knew for certain we were doomed. "I wish I'd brought one of my sister's disgusting sandwiches," I muttered. "That worked last time." As I said the word *wish*, a bubble shape floated out of my mouth with a picture of a stinky cheese sandwich inside. Wish bubbles, like dreams, weren't invisible to Chimes like they were to normal people. The wish floated into the dark sky and popped two seconds later.

"Come on, spread out!" Cryptorum grumbled. "You'll never find the monster when you're bunched together like that. Remember – you have to learn how to look. Otherwise you'll only see what other people want you to."

This was the kind of thing Cryptorum always said. We shuffled nervously along the bank. I drew my sword and poked at a clump of water weed. A faint splash came from the opposite bank.

"I heard something!" I switched back to the torch. Shining it over the water, I noticed ripples sliding smoothly across the surface. I couldn't see any tentacles though. "Mr Cryptorum. . . ?" I looked round but Cryptorum was out of sight. Had he found something or had a monster taken him?

The ripples slid closer and the ground began to shudder.

"Earthquake!" yelled Aiden, grabbing hold of a tree.

"It can't be!" Nora stumbled as the shaking grew stronger. "It must be a wurm – maybe a hell wurm!"

"A hell wurm!" I gulped. "That's not as bad as it sounds, right?"

A colossal black wurm, bigger than a bus, erupted from the ground showering all of us with earth. Its rubbery body oozed with dark slime and its mouth gaped, showing four rings of vicious-looking teeth. A massive crater opened where the monster had tunnelled through and cracks spread across the ground. The wurm swayed back and forth, as if it was tasting the air. Then it lunged straight at me.

"Robyn!" Nora shot an arrow from her bow, aiming so wildly that it sailed right over the wurm's head.

I dodged and ran. The wurm snapped its teeth and I dropped to the ground, letting the creature swing over me. I felt its hot breath on the back of my neck. The stink of rotting flesh made me gag.

"H-hey, wurm!" Aiden stammered, waving his torchblade at the beast. "Over here!"

The wurm swayed, searching for the sound.

"Don't, Aiden! You'll get yourself killed." I scrambled to my feet. My head was pounding. "Where's Cryptorum? We need help!"

Nora shrieked as the wurm charged in her direction. I pressed my torch and the blade shot out, glinting in the lamplight. Could a frostblade pierce the wurm's rubbery hide or would the sword just make the monster more angry? I was about to find out.

Jumping over a huge crater, I launched myself at the wurm. Its head was turned away so I swung at its side and my sword bounced off like a twig hitting a car tyre. The blow sent a jolt down my arm and I stumbled backwards, nearly falling into the crater.

The monster made a "HUH?" sound and swung towards me. Now I was closer I could see a slimy black tongue behind the four rows of spiky teeth. Two mean-looking eyes blinked in the middle of the slimy mess. I mean, what kind of creature has eyes in its *tongue*?

I reached for my bow – planning to fire right at its mouth – but it wasn't on my shoulder any more. I must've dropped it. Backing away, I reached the riverbank. My heart was jumping against my ribs.

Which way should I go – left towards the trees or right towards the car park? I chose left just as the wurm moved, opening a line of cracks on either side of me.

I was trapped.

If my life was a movie, this was the part where Aiden would throw me an awesome new weapon to defeat the monster with. Or I'd suddenly master a flying kick-somersault which would send the wurm diving back underground. Instead I just stood there, gripping my frostblade and trying to ignore my shaking hands.

The wurm swayed a little. I was sure it was enjoying this.

My gaze flicked to the water behind me and then back to the wurm. The river was my only way out, but would I be swapping a wurm for a nesha?

The water rippled. A large animal with a shaggy coat and glowing green eyes leapt out of the river. Baring its teeth at the wurm, the beast let out a volley of barks. A shower of arrows flew across the river, hitting the wurm right in the mouth. The hairy creature barked again and more arrows whizzed over and hit their target.

The wurm writhed. Spitting out arrows, it

swung round and plunged back into the earth. The ground shuddered as it dived deeply and vanished in a shower of mud. I wiped the dirt off my face and raised my sword. What *was* this new monster? It didn't look much like any of the water beasts Nora had shown me in Cryptorum's books.

The creature turned to face me, panting. Then it shook itself fiercely. Water drops flew off its thick coat and splattered all over me.

"Thanks!" I wiped my eyes with my sleeve.

The creature gave a short bark, sat on its haunches and watched me carefully. It was obvious that it wasn't going to eat me – at least not straight away. I packed up my sword and switched my torch back on so I could get a better look at it. The animal's coat was greyish-white and it had a long bushy tail. Its snout was black and its green eyes shone eerily in the torchlight.

Nora picked her way across the broken ground. "Look at those eyes! Do you think it's some kind of super-dog?"

"You don't know what it is then?" I raised my eyebrows. "Haven't you read about it somewhere?"

"There's nothing in Mr Cryptorum's books about a beast with green eyes. Not unless it's among the papers he won't let me see – the ones in the locked archive in the cellar." Edging closer, Nora reached out to touch the creature, but it gave a low growl and she pulled her hand back quickly.

Aiden climbed out of the deep trench left by the hell wurm. His hand shook as he brushed mud off his jacket. "That thing was vicious! I thought wurms were shy and kept out of people's way. I thought that's why we'd never seen one before."

"They are shy – they're supposed to be, anyway," Nora said. "I guess hell wurms are a bit more outgoing than the other wurms."

"I never want to meet one again," Aiden shuddered. "Where did those arrows come from?"

"Must have been Cryptorum." I shone the torch at the blackness around us.

The beast with the green eyes sniffed the air and gave a short bark. A low whirring sound grew into a roar that cut out after a few seconds. A motorized dinghy zoomed into view on the river with a blond-haired boy at the helm and two more figures sitting behind him. My stomach lurched. Not the BUTT kids again. Tristan, Portia and Rufus were the last people I wanted to see when I was covered in earth after nearly being eaten by a wurm. Why couldn't they ever turn up when I was looking like a great Chime fighter with a clean leather jacket and polished frostblade?

"Hello, Robyn! Hi, guys!" Rufus flicked back his blond fringe as he steered the dinghy towards the bank. "You look terrible. You didn't have trouble with a monster, did you?"

I Meet My First Chime Wolf

met Rufus's perfect blue eyes and forced myself to smile. "No trouble here! We were just dodging a hell wurm, that's all."

Portia said something behind her hand and I seethed with annoyance. The BUTT kids were always like this. The letters BUTT stood for Beast Undercover Tracking Taskforce – or so they'd once told us – but to me the name made it obvious *where* they were a great big pain. They trained at Kesterly Manor – the home of Dominic Dray – and they'd been practising to hunt and fight monsters since they were little. Rufus had perfected this sarcastic look every time he wanted to point out how rubbish our equipment was compared with theirs. Portia could be mean and Tristan was just plain moody.

Portia leapt on to the bank, her sleek ponytail swinging, and pulled the dinghy to the shore. Tristan jumped out, his thin face drawn into a frown. Then Rufus strolled on to the bank and paused, hand on hip, like some kind of hero come to save the day. He flicked a button on the metal cylinder and an ultrasonic blade leapt out – pale gold and shimmering. It was meant to be better than the normal frostblades we used, although I'd never really believed it.

Each of the BUTT kids was wearing a shiny black watch that could measure how their body was functioning – heart rate and oxygen level, all that kind of stuff. Dray liked his trainees to have every kind of gadget.

The green-eyed dog pricked up his ears, his eyes fixed on Rufus.

"Is that your dog?" I said.

Rufus put away his ultrasonic blade, smiling smugly. "It isn't a dog. This is our Chime wolf." He turned to the wolf. "Come here, Storm." The wolf leapt to Rufus's side, his tail raised high. "We were given him three days ago by a man from the International Federation of Chimes.

He's great at tracking things, as you can tell with the hell wurm – I reckon we're finding and capturing ten times as many monsters as we used to."

"Doesn't say much for those scanner things you used before," I said, scowling. The Federation guy must have given *them* the last Chime wolf. It was so unfair!

"We still use our scanners too." Rufus's smile never wavered. "You can't have too many gadgets! Oh, I suppose you wouldn't know, would you?"

"Where's *your* wolf?" Portia asked pointedly.

There was a horrible pause. I stared at Storm the wolf and tried to choke back the massive wave of jealousy rolling over me. The wolf had the furriest grey-white coat and its eyes were so intelligent. I'd always wanted a pet and I'd begged Mum and Dad for a dog but they'd always said no. Actually what Dad had said was: *This house is like a zoo already. There's no room for a dog.*

"The Federation had run out, so we didn't get one," Aiden explained.

"Maybe they didn't think you were good enough to have one," Portia sneered.

My face grew hot. "Maybe we're just better at tracking monsters without needing one!"

Portia's eyes narrowed into glittering black points. "MAYBE the Federation knows that *we're* the real Chimes. After all, Kesterly Manor has a combat studio full of amazing equipment and full weather controls. We can train in all conditions – wind, snow, tornado – just at the push of a button."

I glared back. "Well, we don't need that. WE just go outside!" If she flicked her ponytail one more time I was sure I'd strangle her.

"Kesterly Manor has an automated fighting instructor AND an Olympic-sized swimming pool with a diving board AND a mock-up town in the basement!"

"If it's that great why did you leave? If you stayed there all the time then WE wouldn't have to put up with seeing you!"

Portia reached for her ultrasonic blade so I whipped my sword out too. We stood there, eyeballing each other. Slime from the hell wurm glistened on my sword tip.

"Now, now, children!" Dominic Dray came along the riverbank using his cane to pick his way over the cracks in the ground left by the wurm. Cryptorum was just behind him. "In this time of danger we have to try to get along with each other. We can't be quarrelling among ourselves, can we?"

I was tempted to say that Portia had started it but I caught Cryptorum glaring at me and decided to let it go. Dray cast me a mocking look. This was the first time I'd seen him since he'd tried to persuade me to train at Kesterly Manor and I'd refused. I wondered whether he was still angry.

"The beast was a hell wurm, sir," Rufus said to Dray. "I'd hoped we could attach a tracker to its hide and trace where it went, but with the other trainees so close by we had to fire on the monster to prevent them from being injured." His eyes slid in my direction. "We hit the beast in the mouth – its weak point of course – and it retreated quickly."

"Well done, Rufus!" Dray nodded approvingly. "That was a perfect example of how to keep your cool and deal with a monster effectively. I'm sure the other Chimes are grateful."

"Yeah, thanks!" Aiden actually looked like he meant it. "Next time we'll know how to fight those wurms."

Portia smirked and played with her ultrasonic blade, flicking it on and off.

I flushed, thinking of how we'd run about yelling and diving to the ground. At least Cryptorum hadn't seen us.

"This proves it," Cryptorum said to Dray. "Robyn told me about a nesha at the park and I wasn't sure whether to believe it at first. But now ... seeing a hell wurm right here... The Grand Master of the Clocks must be right."

"All the signs point to it," Dray agreed. "But where and when will it rise? We must pool our resources, Erasmus. We have to work together on this."

I pressed the button to collapse my torchblade. I knew they were talking about the big beast that was meant to appear sometime soon and I was surprised Cryptorum wanted Dray's advice. He hadn't exactly been helpful when a vampire threatened Wendleton last winter.

"Why is the Federation so sure the big monster will show up here?" I blurted out. "And if they know it's coming why don't they know what it is?"

Rufus and Portia grinned while Tristan looked at me as if I was mad.

"Weren't you listening to the man from the Federation yesterday?" Cryptorum barked. "They measured a spike in dark energy in this area. The Grand Master has a circle of clocks, each one the twin of a Mortal Clock somewhere round the world. He must have matched the dark energy he detected to the Grimdean clock."

Dray nodded. "He matched it to the Grimdean clock and to the Kesterly clock too. As our towns are close together, the Master deduced that this new threat could rise anywhere in the area. There is no way to tell what it will be. It could be anything from a flesh-shrivelling caderwack to a wraith with iron eyes."

I pictured the Master of the Clocks sitting alone in the centre of a circle of ticking clocks, each one a twin of a Mortal Clock somewhere far away. "So when we see this creature we might not know it's the big monster we've been waiting for?"

"It'll be more dangerous than anything else you've seen," Dray said, seriously. "I don't think you'll be able to miss it."

"But—" I began, before Cryptorum frowned me into silence.

The two men turned aside, talking between themselves for a moment. Dray broke off to call to the BUTT kids. "Take the boat downstream. I'll meet you at the bridge."

Rufus held the boat steady while the others climbed in. "See you later, Grimdeaners!" He grinned, showing perfect teeth. Then, with a short burst of the motor, the boat glided away. The Chime wolf bounded along the riverbank beside them, muscles rippling beneath its thick fur. Portia glared back at me till they disappeared into the dark.

"Meet me in the car park, you three," Cryptorum said, dismissing us quickly.

"They get to monster-hunt by boat!" Aiden sighed as we picked our way up the riverbank. "You've got to admit, they have great stuff."

"The things you invent are much more unique," Nora said loyally. "And you've worked on them by yourself. They just get gadgets handed to them."

I hung back and let Nora and Aiden go ahead. Cryptorum and Dray were deep in conversation and I wanted to know what they were saying. I knew eavesdropping wasn't a good thing to do but I didn't trust Dray since he tried to tempt me away from Grimdean to join his trainees last winter. Jumping into a trench left by the hell wurm, I crept closer.

"So what did he say?" Dray was leaning forward on his cane. "Didn't he understand that you've only been training these children since last autumn? They've hardly had time to acquire any skills."

I bristled. That showed what Dray knew. I had

plenty of skill! But my heart sank as Cryptorum answered. "The Grand Master of the Clocks is not an understanding man. He said if their skills really were as basic as I described, I should give up training them right now. He's sending Fettle back in two weeks to assess them. If they fail, they'll be banned from fighting for ever and I'll be back to hunting monsters alone."

Dray put a hand on Cryptorum's shoulder. "You wouldn't be alone, Erasmus. Truly. . ."

I stumbled back along the ditch, a hollow feeling in my stomach. How could Cryptorum say that about us? Our skills weren't basic. I swallowed, thinking of our failure to beat the hell wurm. But that was just because we hadn't seen one before. . .

"What's wrong?" Nora asked, as I reached the car park.

I shook my head. "Nothing!"

"Right, you lot!" Cryptorum loomed out of the darkness. "I'm sending you back while I stay and look for that nesha."

"Why can't we stay and help?" My face flamed. "I bet Dray would let his Chime kids. Aren't we good enough or something?"

Cryptorum looked at me under his bushy eyebrows. "I know you don't like those children –

and I haven't forgotten what happened with Dominic last winter – but we need him this time." His forehead creased into deep lines. "This surge in dark energy is a more serious threat than anything we've faced before. We must share information. So you're just going to have to get on with those other Chime kids."

"Does that mean we'll see them again soon?" Nora asked.

"It does," Cryptorum said grimly. "We're going to visit them at Kesterly Manor."

Pudding Arrives at Grimdean House

t took me a long time to get to sleep that night. I kept turning over, trying to get comfortable, while Cryptorum's words whirled around my head more wildly than a nesha's tentacles.

He's sending Fettle back in two weeks to assess them. If they fail, they'll be banned from fighting for ever...

Why hadn't Cryptorum told the Grand Master of the Clocks that we were doing great with our training? I frowned, thinking of Nora and Aiden. I had to admit that though we were all good at something, none of us was great at everything. My sword skills were really strong, Aiden was good at inventing awesome stuff and Nora knew more monster facts than the rest of us put together. Should I tell them both what Cryptorum said to Dray last night? Maybe I shouldn't. Nora already had very little confidence in her own sword skills. News of someone coming to test us all would make it worse.

Maybe I could help us all improve in the two weeks we had left. Maybe I could turn us all into perfect Chimes. My brain filled with a dreamy fog.

Maybe we could beat the BUTT kids too. They weren't so tough without their gadgets. . .

When I woke the next morning, I'd been dreaming I was at Kesterly Manor. The truth was I'd been wondering what the place was like for ages. My brain had gone crazy, turning the dream manor into a creepy funfair with monsters stalking the rides. I was driving a go-kart with a grodder chasing me and flattening every kart it passed with its hairy bull-like body. As I fled for my life, a man with a bowler hat labelled FEDERATION stood at the side shaking his head and making notes on a clipboard.

In the dream I'd gone searching for something – a weapon maybe – that would help me fight all the monsters in one go. I'd been approaching the weapons shed, sure that it would have the special object I needed inside. Then Rufus, Portia and Tristan had come along with their super-cool, green-eyed wolf and told me they didn't like me and I should go away.

I woke up, blinking, and stared at the ceiling, which was striped with daylight shining over the top of the curtains. Annie was still sleeping in the bed opposite, which was strange because normally she was awake and jumping up and down on me by six-thirty. A silver moth fluttered past my face and I reached up to capture it. I hardly ever saw my own dream moths – they disappeared so fast when I woke. Carefully, I opened my fingers and the silvery moth waved its antennae indignantly.

"Sorry!" I said. "I just wanted to look at you."

"Who are you talking to?" Annie sat up in bed and stuck her thumb in the corner of her mouth.

"Um . . . no one. Just a bug." The moth flew out of my hand – blue, gold and green flashing on its wings – but I knew Annie wouldn't be able to see it. It wasn't surprising that this moth had brought me a dream about Kesterly. I remembered thinking about Dominic Dray and going to visit the place before I fell asleep.

"Show me!" Annie scrambled out of bed and ran over just as the dream moth flickered into nothing.

"It's gone!" I showed her my empty hands. "We'd better get to breakfast."

"Robyn? Annie?" Mum was standing at the bottom of the stairs as I came down. "There you are! Can you wake Sammie up, please? It's nearly seven-thirty already. You're all going to be late."

Groaning, I climbed back upstairs and banged on Sammie's bedroom door. "Wake up, lazy!" There was no answer. Sighing, I opened the door. Going into Sammie's room was more dangerous than facing the hell wurm. "Sammie, wake up!"

Sammie gave a grunting, snuffling sound. She was all tangled up with her duvet covering most of her face. Twenty awesome ways to wake her up crossed my mind. Where was my water gun?

"Robyn? Sammie?" Mum called from below.

I was about to shake my sister's shoulder when something black crawled across her pillow. I jumped, thinking it was a spider. The black thing crawled up Sammie's neck and on to her hair. Raising its dark metallic wings, it took off.

"Jeez!" I ducked as the thing flew at my face. Tripping over a pile of clothes on the floor, I lost my balance and clutched at the bed.

"What the heck?" Sammie looked at me blearily. "Robyn, GET OUT of my room!"

"Where'd it go?" I scrambled up and caught sight of the bug circling the lampshade. Suddenly it burst into a tiny ball of grey fog before fading into nothing. "OK, that was weird."

Sammie hit me round the head with her pillow and I staggered sideways. Another black bug crawled up her shoulder and that one burst into grey fog before vanishing too.

I dodged to avoid another blow from the pillow. "Mum sent me to wake you up. Look, I'm going!"

"Don't come in my room EVER AGAIN!" Sammie shouted.

I slammed the door shut and leaned against the other side. Those bugs were from the Unseen World for sure. Nothing normal burst into little pockets of fog like that. So what were they? And why were they hanging around Sammie?

"I know what they are. I saw them for the first time a few months ago," Aiden said, when I told him about the weird bugs at school that day.

It was lunchtime and we were sitting by a wall in the Grimdean garden. Aiden had chosen the spot because we were mostly hidden from view and he wanted to work on his new gadget without anyone bothering him. I was busy watching Mrs Lovell, our headmistress, telling off a bunch of younger kids who'd gone to play tag in the statue garden. After the roof had fallen in and Ashbrook school had moved to Grimdean House, Cryptorum had roped off a large area of his lawn to be the playground and sports field. Outside this rope were a bunch of tempting places: the creepy statue garden, the hiding places behind the fir trees at the bottom of the garden and the huge wooden shed on the right known as the bat barn.

Everyone had been really excited about the bat barn at first – trying to creep in and get a peek at the rows and rows of bats hanging upside down from the rafters. These days nobody took any notice if the bats came out and swooped round the garden. Me, Nora and Aiden were the only ones who knew that Cryptorum kept them to track monsters of course, but having a hundred bats in his back garden added to Cryptorum's reputation for being totally weird.

"Go on then! What are they?" I demanded. "Some kind of spooky fog beetles?"

"They're nightmares – they disappear really quickly like the dream moths do." Aiden fiddled with the wiring inside a little metal box. He took a small screwdriver out of his pocket. "Nora told me they're called dream leeches. They were black with dark shiny wings, right?"

I pictured the nasty-looking bugs. "Yeah, that's right. They were on Sammie's pillow when she woke up." I paused. I'd never thought that my older sister could have nightmares. To me, she WAS the nightmare.

Aiden tightened the screws on the metal box. I had no idea what he was making this time. Often he wouldn't explain what he was doing till it was finished.

"How long have you known about them?" I asked. "You never said anything before."

Aiden rubbed his thick hair. "I got nightmares for a couple of weeks after that fight at Blagdurn Heath before Christmas and one time I woke up and saw the dream leeches flying round me. I told Nora – she'd had nightmares so she'd seen them too."

I stared. Aiden was my best friend but he hadn't told me any of this. "Were they bad – the nightmares?"

"Nah!" He shrugged. "Just the usual being-chased-by-monsters kind of thing." He held up the metal box. "I'm inventing something that can track creatures of the Unseen World by giving out sonic waves just like the bats do. I think it'll work better than the Kesterly kids' subthermal scanner because that uses heat and some monsters don't have much body heat, especially if they're cold-blooded."

"Sounds great!" I said, surprised by the sudden change of subject. "If it's ready by tonight we can test it out together. Course, we wouldn't have to build our own scanner if the International Federation of Chimes hadn't given their last wolf to Rufus and the others."

Aiden put the screwdriver back in his pocket. "I can't wait to see what gadgets they have at the manor."

"Like Nora said – yours are way better."

"Course, you could have trained there if you'd wanted to – with Dray offering you a place." Aiden gave a half-smile which made me wonder whether he was jealous that I'd been asked and he hadn't.

"I wouldn't have said yes to that in a million years. . ."

"Hey!" Nora ran up to us. "Have you guys seen Mr Cryptorum today? I think he wants a really long training session this evening but my parents want me home by six so they can spend time helping me with my homework."

I rolled my eyes sympathetically. Nora's parents were high school teachers and were always getting her to do extra schoolwork at home.

"I don't think I can stay late either," Aiden said.

I hesitated. Should I tell them about what Cryptorum had said yesterday to Dominic Dray? "I think we need the extra training time. Last night, just before we left—"

The bell rang for the end of lunchtime setting off a screeching wail from the scree sags locked in the dungeon. I winced even though I was used to it. The rest of the school poured off the Grimdean lawn, totally unaware of the noise.

"I'll tell you later," I said to the others as we were swept up by the tide of kids rushing inside.

I was halfway to our classroom when I heard excited shrieks at the front of the crowd. The herd of kids by the entrance hall came to a halt and everyone behind them started shoving as they tried to see what was happening.

"No pushing, children! Everyone go to your classrooms at once," cried Mrs Lovell in her best headmistress manner but no one took any notice.

Miss Smiting appeared in the front entrance, her eyes flashing. "Sssilence!" She ended with a long hiss. "Mr Cryptorum doess not like a commotion. Everyone to classs right now." All the kids stopped pushing and hurried towards their classrooms. Mrs Lovell followed them, flapping her hands as if she was shooing chickens.

Miss Smiting caught sight of me and Aiden and beckoned us over. There was an odd yelping sound which made my heart flip over. I squeezed past the last few little kids to find an enormous dog with thick honey-white fur padding round the entrance hall. He had big brown eyes like melted chocolate. "Wow, he's amazing. Is he yours? Are you keeping him?" I bent down to stroke the dog, and his coat was thick and soft under my fingers.

Miss Smiting smiled. "No, but you are! I have found you a Chime wolf."

"Are you sure that's a wolf?" Aiden said doubtfully. "The simple fact is, it doesn't look the same as the Kesterly one."

Miss Smiting dismissed Aiden's doubts with a wave of her hand. "His mother wass a wolf. I guess there could be other bloodlines too – a bit of golden retriever perhapss – but he has been trained by a Chime and he knows what to do."

"He's awesome!" I grinned and ruffled the wolf's coat.

"Junella, what on earth—" Cryptorum stomped downstairs and climbed awkwardly over the rope hanging across the bottom of the staircase which was there to stop nosy kids sneaking up to his private rooms. "Where has that animal come from? Don't tell me one of the children brought their dog to school!"

"No, Erasmuss!" Miss Smiting checked the corridors were empty before continuing. "This is a Chime wolf for Robyn, Aiden and Nora. I got the train all the way to Holyhead to visit Biden Jones. I knew he'd ssell me a wolf if I could talk to him in person." Her eyes gleamed.

Miss Smiting had a knack for persuading people. It was a snake-woman skill and it seemed to happen when she fixed her green eyes with thin black pupils on someone. Unfortunately it didn't always work on Cryptorum.

"You've been fooled!" he snapped. "That's not a Chime wolf. I'll have Biden's head for this!"

The wolf barked sharply at Cryptorum as if it knew exactly what he was saying. A door clicked and Mrs Lovell hurried out of a nearby classroom. "Oh, excuse me! But is that creature yours? It's just that there's an Ashbrook rule not to have dogs at school."

Cryptorum drew himself up as if his chest was filling with steam. "Really? It's an Ashbrook school rule, is it?"

"Yes, I'm afraid so." The headmistress twisted her necklace nervously.

"Well!" The word burst from Cryptorum. "It's a Grimdean rule that no one tells me what to do in my own house." Mrs Lovell wilted under his glare. "So the wo... I mean the dog is going to stay!"

The headmistress muttered something and scurried away. I couldn't stop a grin spreading over my face. The wolf was going to stay!

"We can test his tracking skills tonight!" Aiden was grinning too. "Thanks for buying him, Miss Smiting."

Cryptorum grunted, climbed over the rope and stomped back upstairs. Miss Smiting gave us a wink. "You're welcome, my dearsss."

I beamed. Surely the Federation couldn't stop us from being Chimes now that we actually had a Chime wolf?

"His coat's exactly the same shade as the pastry on my mum's pies," Aiden said. "She does apple ones and cherry ones – they're my favourite kind of pudding."

"Then that's what we should call him." I hugged the wolf. "We'll name you Pudding."

6

I Get Spaghettified

udding became an instant celebrity at Grimdean House and Miss Smiting had to literally pull children off him when the bell rang for the end of the school day. Luckily he was a really friendly animal. He didn't even mind when some of the younger ones tried to ride him, though Cryptorum put a stop to that straight away.

"Pudding's a silly name if you think about it." Aiden tightened the string on his bow. "I think we should call him Vortex."

We were standing at the bottom of the Grimdean garden after school waiting for Cryptorum to bring things out of the weapons shed.

"It's not silly! Like you said – his coat is the

exact colour of pie crust. Anyway, Vortex sounds like Storm – the name of Kesterly wolf." I spotted Nora racing down the lawn. "Hey, Nora! Come and meet our Chime wolf. I've called him Pudding – don't you think it's a great name?"

"Is he really ours?" Nora's eyes shone. "Look at that golden fur. I think Pudding suits him."

"If you yell the word *wolf* any louder, Robyn Silver, my neighbours will hear and call the police." Cryptorum's head appeared through a hole in the shed floor that I didn't even know existed. "Now are you going to stand there yakking all afternoon or are you going to help me with this equipment?"

Aiden rushed over to help Cryptorum lift a big black box through the hole. I tried to get a good look down the opening but Cryptorum and the ladder blocked the way. What was he hiding down there? I should have known the weapons shed wasn't just a shed – nothing was normal at Grimdean. Maybe his best weapons were down there, or something so dangerous he didn't want us to touch it.

I grabbed one end of the black box, which weighed a tonne, and shuffled backwards, trying to keep pace with Aiden. The box banged against the door frame.

"Careful!" Cryptorum warned. "Now set it down over there."

"Is it a ghetto blaster?" Nora said excitedly. "My dad has one of those."

"What's a ghetto blaster? Does it blast monsters?" I scanned the sides of the box as we lowered it to the ground. There was a row of metal dials along the top and a round shape covered with weird black mesh on one side. Pudding sniffed the box suspiciously and gave a soft growl.

"They played music on them in the eighties. My dad says everyone used to carry them round on their shoulders," Nora said with a giggle. "My dad's has a handle though and more dials."

Cryptorum frowned us into silence. "We are entering a new stage of your training." He paused for a long time and the hairs rose on the back of my neck. "I'd intended to leave all this until you had gained more fighting skills but now that we have this new threat, it cannot wait."

Nora twiddled her plait nervously. Aiden was staring fixedly at the black box.

"All monsters give out a trail of dark energy which cannot be seen with the human eye, and the more dangerous the monster the more dark energy they leave behind." Cryptorum glared round, checking we were listening. "The Federation aren't the only ones who can detect this energy. I devised my own way of doing it many years ago. I'm trusting you all to keep this information to yourselves – I wouldn't be very popular with the Federation if they knew I'd made my own machine." He knelt down beside the black box, flicked a switch on the side and started turning the dials on the top.

I grinned. I liked the idea of Cryptorum being a rebel. "Serves them right for trying to order everyone around."

Cryptorum twisted the last dial and a spluttery, whistling noise came from the machine. Pudding pricked up his ears and whined. "So this is my Dark Energy Detector. I call it the DED for short. I wanted you to learn to track monsters using your own senses, with some help from the bats of course, but now something big is about to rise so we must use every tool at our disposal. Don't forget: you mustn't *ever* get too close to this machine while it's switched on. It could be very hazardous."

Aiden crouched beside Cryptorum, buzzing with excitement. "This is exactly the gadget I've been trying to make for the last few days!"

"It took me months to put this together back in 1994," Cryptorum grunted. "I don't have your skill with inventions of course. It doesn't look very pretty but it works."

"But ... detecting dark energy isn't in any of your books, and I've read just about everything in your study," Nora cried.

"I keep certain books locked up in the basement," Cryptorum replied, drawing the closest thing I'd ever seen to a scowl out of Nora. "I didn't want you going out and trying to detect dark energy without me. If you get the settings on the DED wrong the result can be very nasty." He bent an ear towards the black-meshed circle. A crackling sound burst through like an out-of-tune radio and he quickly started twisting dials.

"But what about Pudding?" I put in. "He's going to help us track monsters so why do we need this machine as well?"

"The wolf – if it really is a wolf – can only track one monster at a time," Cryptorum told me. "The DED detects the dark energy *all* monsters leave behind so it can pinpoint places with a heavy concentration of the stuff. It's our best chance of finding the powerful new monster that's going to rise. With care and luck, we can stop this beast before it reaches a street full of people and does real damage."

Pudding's ears pricked up as some bats swooped out of the bat barn and circled overhead. I sighed. I'd really wanted to search for monsters with Pudding tonight. What was the point in finally having a Chime wolf if you didn't take him out hunting?

The hiss of static grew into a loud shriek and Cryptorum flicked a switch to turn the machine off. "It's showing a mass of dark energy in the shed, which is nonsense of course. It must be picking up traces of monster fur and spines on some of the frostblades. We'll get a better reading if we switch it on away from here."

I rolled my eyes. Was he saying the machine wasn't even working properly?

Aiden ran his fingers over the black dials. "Does it work by detecting the frequency of the dark energy – like it's a signal?"

"Indeed it does." Cryptorum picked up the whole box and rested it on his shoulder. "And with any luck we'll track down the place in Wendleton with the most dark energy. Follow me!" He strode away across the garden.

I patted my side and called softly for Pudding.

I wasn't leaving him behind no matter what Cryptorum said.

Nora ran inside to collect a bug jar and a net so that we looked like a proper nature club. Then we walked through Wendleton using the back streets. Every few paces, Cryptorum switched on the DED and bent his ear to listen to the crackling and whining. Nora and Aiden discussed the machine in excited whispers but I didn't understand much of what they were saying.

"It probably uses a temporal oscillator powered by electrical pulses," Nora murmured.

"That doesn't explain why the machine's producing such strong audible feedback," Aiden replied. "If you think about it, there's no indication of an alternating current."

The DED made an especially loud shriek and Cryptorum turned on to a patch of scrubland just beyond a supermarket car park. "This place looks promising. The dark energy readings are high which means something very dangerous has been here recently – it could still be in the area."

Growling, Pudding bounded across the strip of waste ground and pulled a short, spiky creature out of the hedge.

"Pudding's caught a kobold already. I knew he'd

be awesome!" I grinned, watching the Chime wolf tussle with the fierce little thing that looked like a goblin crossed with a porcupine. Kobolds were the one of the ugliest creatures of the Unseen World but also one of the least dangerous, though the spines covering their bodies could leave you with some nasty cuts.

"Control that wolf! I'm trying to concentrate," Cryptorum barked. "The DED has detected something much worse than a little kobold."

I called Pudding back and the kobold bolted across the car park and hid behind a tower of empty crates near the supermarket's back door.

Cryptorum set the machine down and fiddled with its dials until he got the same dull whine as before. Then he dusted off his hands in a satisfied way and stared round as if he was expecting something to appear.

"What happens next?" I asked.

"Shh!" Cryptorum frowned. "You must listen for any change in the machine's sound."

I fidgeted with my torchblade. Pudding's nose was twitching and he kept looking at the hedge and then back at me. He must have detected more kobolds in there. I sighed. This was just a waste of time. The man from the Federation would be back in two weeks to test us and we wouldn't be ready. I had to tell Aiden. I nudged him.

"Stop it, Robyn!" he hissed.

No one moved. In the distance, cars vroomed in and out of the supermarket car park. Then there was a POP! It was so clear it was almost like a sound effect on TV.

"That's the highest energy reading!" Cryptorum flicked the machine off. "There must be a monster very close. . ."

"Which direction is it?" Nora asked.

"It's hard to say." Cryptorum scanned the place. "Just keep your eyes open."

"Why don't we use the DED to work out the direction?" I said, but everyone else was too busy rushing from one end of the waste ground to the other to take any notice. I spotted a dark shape behind a tree. Was that a monster?

The others were all at the far side of the waste ground, looking in the wrong direction, so I decided I'd use the DED to show them what I'd found. Crouching down, I flicked the switch on the side of the machine and faint crackling burst out of it. I fiddled with the dials on the top. I didn't really know what I was doing but I was sure it couldn't be that hard.

I picked up the DED and moved towards the dark shape I'd spotted. Suddenly a new sound came from the machine – a purring sound. That had to be a good sign!

"I've found something!" I set the machine down, calling to the others in a loud whisper. "Hear that? It has to mean something big." I pointed to the circle of black mesh and a strange force gripped my finger. I was pulled closer to the machine, my heels skidding on the grass. It felt as if my finger was caught in a monster's jaws.

"Robyn! I said don't get too close to the machine when it's switched on." Cryptorum was beside me in a second. Gripping my arm, he tried pulling me backwards but it made no difference.

My finger throbbed, as if it was being squeezed and pulled all at the same time. Then my heart stopped for a second. Was my finger getting longer?

Like a little pink sausage, my finger stretched and stretched. Then my whole hand stretched. Even my arm seemed to be getting longer.

Nora made a horrified moan, her hand over her mouth. Pudding crouched down, snapping at the machine.

"What do we do?" Aiden shouted to Cryptorum. "We have to do something!"

"All we can do is hope the energy reverses," Cryptorum puffed, still trying to pull me backwards. "Because if it doesn't. . ."

Suddenly the pressure on my hand released, leaving my massively long finger waggling in mid-air. There was a tiny pause before a blast of wind stronger than a high-speed train blasted from the DED and knocked me over. Cryptorum twisted the dials frantically. A fuzzy static sound poured from the machine, cutting out as Cryptorum flicked the off switch.

I felt kind of dizzy. It didn't help that my finger was longer than a string of spaghetti. "What do I do? The machine got me!" I waggled my finger and it wobbled like jelly. Why was my finger so bendy – wasn't the bone still in there?

"Ew!" Nora gazed in fascination. "It's like olden days when they put prisoners on the rack. Look, your arm is twice as long as the other one."

Cryptorum chuckled.

"It's not funny!" I tried to turn and walk off but I nearly smacked Aiden round the face with my noodle finger. "I saw the shape of a big monster right behind that tree. That's the only reason I touched the machine. It's probably still there!" As I finished, a cat jumped out from behind the tree and ran away.

Cryptorum laughed even harder.

Aiden stared at my finger. "That's what happens when something meets a black hole in outer space. I watched a TV programme about it. Whatever falls into the hole just stretches and stretches as it gets sucked in. It's called spaghettification."

Cryptorum's shoulders were shaking. "You know Robyn, it doesn't look that bad ... and having such a long finger could be handy for reaching things on high shelves."

"Stop laughing!" I said. "I can't live with a hand like this!"

Nora and Aiden started giggling too. "At least when you point at something people will really take notice!" Aiden joked.

"IT'S NOT FUNNY!" I yelled. "Just because you think we're going to fail the Federation test doesn't mean you can give up on us!"

Nora put a hand on my arm. "Robyn, it's shrinking. See!"

It was weird watching the whole thing in reverse. My finger grew fatter and shorter and my whole hand lost its thin, stretched look. A few seconds later I was back to normal. I wiggled my fingers just to make sure.

When I glanced up, they were all staring at me.

Nora and Aiden looked confused. Cryptorum was glaring at me from under his eyebrows.

"What test are you talking about?" Aiden asked.

"Nothing good comes to people who eavesdrop on conversations they're not meant to hear, Robyn," Cryptorum growled. "You always rush into things without thinking. If you'd been sucked in by the DED for much longer your whole body would have stretched and you might have stayed that way." He picked up the machine. "I don't know what I was thinking, showing you this. You're not ready."

"You don't trust us! You don't think we're good enough," I snapped.

Cryptorum stomped away with the machine under his arm and it was Aiden's turn to glare at me.

"I heard him talking to Dominic Dray last night," I said to Aiden and Nora. "That man from the Federation is coming back to test us and if we fail they won't let us be Chimes any more. We have to practise harder and get better at everything."

"Cryptorum will train us – he'll make sure we don't fail." Aiden frowned. "This isn't just about you. I really wanted to learn how the DED works and you just ruined it. You didn't even care what he was showing us."

"I'm sorry!" I shoved my back-to-normal-size hands in my pockets.

"Maybe when we go to Kesterly Manor we can pick up some training tips from Rufus and the others and that'll help us to pass," Nora said.

I caught my breath. "What? We're taking tips off the BUTT kids now?"

"Well they knew how to battle the hell wurm. Maybe we can learn something from them." Nora shrugged.

For a second I couldn't think of anything to say. The BUTT kids had never been better than us. They'd been training longer – sure – and they had all those gadgets. But they weren't better.

I watched Nora and Aiden follow Cryptorum. Weren't they worried about not being allowed to fight monsters any more? I wasn't going to let any of us fail if I could help it.

"Pudding!" I called and the Chime wolf came trotting over. As we reached the edge of the waste ground, I noticed two black bugs creeping up a lamp post. "Look, Pudding. Dream leeches."

Pudding growled at them.

I suddenly wondered who the nightmares

belonged to. We weren't close to any houses and it was still daylight – why would anyone be sleeping at this time of the afternoon? Unless they'd fallen asleep in front of the TV like Dad often did.

The black beetles vanished one by one in tiny puffs of smoke. Pudding gave a satisfied bark and scampered after the others. After that I kept thinking I saw dream leeches out of the corner of my eyes but every time I turned to look there was nothing there.

Items on Loan

Library name: Lurgan Library
User name: Miss Justine Neill

Author: Harrison, Paula,
Title: The darkest dream
Item ID: C902159284
Date due: 2/11/2019,23:59
Date charged: 12/10/2019,
9:45

We Go to Kesterly Manor

I wanted to take Pudding home with me that evening but I knew Mum and Dad would never let me bring him inside. When I climbed the stairs to Cryptorum's study after school the next day, I was surprised to find a brand-new doggie bed lined with cushions by the fireplace.

Nora nudged me and whispered, "Miss Smiting says Mr Cryptorum went to the pet store and chose it himself."

I pushed down a pang of jealousy. If I couldn't keep Pudding then it was good that Cryptorum was looking after him properly. The wolf was sitting by the window, the sunlight catching on his golden coat.

Cryptorum marched in with Aiden behind him. "Downstairs to the car! We're going to Kesterly Manor."

My stomach dropped. "But what about training? If the man from the Federation is coming back in two weeks then. . ."

"We have to find and destroy this new monster before it endangers people's lives. *That* is what's important and sharing information with Mr Dray will help us do it." Cryptorum held the door open. "Hurry up, please."

It was hard to argue when he said it like that, but I couldn't helping asking, "Isn't Kesterly kind of far away? What about dinner?"

"We'll be eating dinner there." Cryptorum hurried us down the stairs.

"What do you think they'll give us for dinner?" I whispered to Nora and Aiden as we settled on the back seat of the limo with Pudding curled up at our feet.

"I don't know!" Aiden rolled his eyes. "Is that the only thing you think about?"

"It's not the *only* thing I think about but it is pretty important," I muttered. "I doubt Mr Dray likes pizza."

I caught Miss Smiting's eye in the car mirror

and a smile twitched on her lips. "No, Robyn, I have absolutely no idea what dish they will sserve for dinner."

I sometimes forgot what good hearing she had. I fell silent, watching the streets and houses flick past the car window. We climbed the steep valley outside of town and headed down the other side, passing a couple of villages and lots of fields and farms. Pudding got up and rested his head on my knee so I rubbed the thick fur behind his ears.

Turning off the main road, we drove down a narrow lane between tall rows of conifers. Grand black gates opened automatically to let us through and then I got my first view of Kesterly Manor. The place was huge, even bigger than Grimdean, with arched windows and a row of thin red chimneys along the roof. In front of the house was an ordinary lawn and drive. I guessed all the interesting stuff – the Chime equipment – was hidden round the back out of sight.

We drew up alongside the front door and Miss Smiting exchanged looks with Cryptorum. "I shall await you here. Pudding can stay with me."

I was about to protest but Miss Smiting gave me one of her sharp looks. As I trailed behind Cryptorum, a hollow feeling grew in my stomach.

After the way me and Portia had argued the last time we met, I couldn't see this visit ending well.

The door swung open. Dominic Dray was leaning on his silver-topped cane, a slight smirk on his face. "Welcome to my humble dwelling! I'm so honoured that you've come."

At first, I thought Kesterly Manor was going to be just like Grimdean – big, old rooms full of china teapots and sofas that looked a hundred years old. The rooms on either side of the front door were just like that, but halfway along the corridor everything changed. The wooden panelling on the walls became smooth orange paint. The floor became silver and a large round pipe was suspended from the ceiling. It was as if someone had flown an alien space station down to Earth and bolted it to the back of the house. I stared up at the ceiling pipe. What the heck was it for?

Dray and Cryptorum shook hands and headed into the sitting room. "Let them show you round," Cryptorum told us, "and be nice!" he added, looking sharply at me.

"Hi, guys." Rufus was leaning against the stairs, his blond hair swept to one side. Tristan muttered something in his ear as we came in. Portia folded her arms and narrowed her eyes.

I was so busy staring at the weird pipe that I missed a step where the floor changed from normal to space station so I tripped and went flying. Scrambling up, I could feel my face going red. Why did I have to do something embarrassing Every Time I met the BUTT kids?

"Nice trip, Robyn?" Portia grinned widely.

"Ha ha!" I snapped. "Never heard that one before."

"Are you all right, Robyn?" Rufus didn't wait for an answer. "We've got loads to show you. Oh, by the way, is there anything you especially want for dinner? We always choose whatever we want."

"You mean your cook makes separate meals for everyone? Seriously?" I stared.

"Wow, you're so lucky!" Nora said. "I'd like sweet and sour chicken with noodles, please."

"Mm." Aiden tilted his head to one side. "Sausages, chips and beans, please."

"Pepperoni pizza!" I said quickly. "Thanks!"

Rufus picked up a pad of paper and a pen from the hall table and scribbled down our food orders. Then he stood under the pipe holding the paper above his head. There was a sudden rush of air and for a second Rufus's hair stood on end. Then the paper flew out of his fingers and disappeared up the silver pipe.

Rufus grinned. "It's a quick way to get our orders in."

"I guess there's a servant at the other end being hit with bits of paper?" I asked.

Rufus ignored this. "So these are all the normal rooms – the dining room, billiards room, library, drawing room. . ." He nodded towards the normal-looking rooms near the entrance.

Nora drifted towards the library, a dreamy expression in her eyes. "So many books!"

I grabbed her arm before she disappeared inside and never came out again.

"And down here is where we train." Rufus led us down the alien space station corridor.

I put my hand on the smooth orange wall and nearly yelped when my fingers sank in a little. It was like touching modelling dough. "Feel the wall!" I whispered to Aiden, but he just shook his head at me.

"This is our gym." Rufus opened the door to a massive gymnasium. Ropes hung from the ceiling. There were vaulting horses, trampolines and a huge climbing wall at the far end. "But the best bit's in here." He led us into a large, well-organized weapons store with holders full of silver swords and racks of bows and arrows. I pulled out one of the frostblades and tried it out. On a special shelf lay three metal cylinders. Aiden pounced on the ultrasonic blades straight away, switching on the pale gold blade and studying it closely.

"Borrow whatever you like." Rufus nodded at the racks of equipment. "And bring it into the combat studio." He zipped up an armoured jacket, chose a sword and swung it in a circle before heading through another door opposite.

The next hall was smaller with weird green walls, the colour of cabbage, and no windows. At the far end was a silver machine that looked suspiciously like a mini cannon.

"What are those for?" Aiden pointed to the odd gaps that made the ceiling look a bit like a cheese grater.

"This place has all-weather training," Tristan boasted. "Snow, hail, storm – we can train in any weather without ever going outside."

"We can show you that later. There's something else you've got to see first." Rufus was grinning all over his face. "Activate Wendy!"

"Wendy is activated!" a smooth voice replied. A door in the corner swung open and a huge girl robot, taller than an adult, with thick arms and legs, clomped into the room. Her skin had a plastic sheen and the curly brown hair hanging down to her waist reminded me of a doll's. She was carrying a frostblade and wearing a red shirt and jeans, big black boots and a cowboy hat.

"This is Wendy – our automated fighting instructor." Rufus was almost hopping up and down with delight.

"Awesome!" Aiden gazed up at the robot as if she was some kind of miracle. "How is she powered?"

"We charge her up each night by plugging her in," Portia said, exchanging little smiles with Tristan.

"So awesome!" Aiden repeated. "She must have a huge circuit board – I'd love to see it."

I rolled my eyes. Aiden had always been mad about gadgets but Wendy definitely looked more freaky than awesome to me. I reckoned the BUTT kids would try to make us fight her next and that was guaranteed to go *really* badly.

"So who wants to fight her first?" Rufus asked.

I knew it. This was a sneaky move – just typical of Rufus. Unfortunately Nora had chosen that moment to scratch her head and her arm was up in the air.

"OK, Nora wants to go first!" Rufus grinned. "Then Aiden, then Robyn. Wendy, activate fight sequence."

"Wait! I didn't. . ." Nora dropped her frostblade and scrambled to pick it up again. "I wasn't volunteering. . ."

Wendy gave a deep bow. "Fight sequence activated."

"Don't worry, you'll be fine!" Rufus said, backing away.

I glared at him. I knew this was a set up by the BUTT kids but I didn't want to take over Nora's fight. "Go, Nora!" I tried to sound encouraging. "Remember your blocking moves."

Wendy twirled her sword like a dancing baton and moved in to strike. Nora blocked the first blow but the second hit her hard and she fell to her knees. Her face creased up and she clutched her arm.

"Hey!" I jumped in, stopping Wendy's next strike. "This isn't fair! Nora didn't have any time to prepare. Let me fight!"

"Robyn, it's my turn next," Aiden put in.

"I know! I'm just saying – I'm ready." As ready as I ever could be for being flattened by a robot called Wendy. I pushed Nora out the way and dodged a blow aimed at my head.

"How about changing her settings? That should help." Portia jumped forwards and pressed something on Wendy's back. At once Robot Girl went crazy, her blows coming twice as fast as before.

"How-does-that-help?" I squawked, ducking and parrying at super speed.

"Oh, sorry! Wrong button." Portia laughed. "How about some different weather to make it more interesting?" She clapped her hands and called, "Mountains in the snow!"

The green walls flickered and a mountain-scape appeared with a high peak and a steep drop to the valley floor. I was admiring how real it looked when a ton of cold white flakes poured from the ceiling and I slipped over.

Wendy stood tall. "Activate snow spikes," she intoned, and thick metal points sprouted on the bottom of her boots. She strode towards me, her feet gripping easily on the icy surface.

"Hey, that's not fair!" I rolled out of the way as her blade hit the snow where my head had been. Hurriedly, I scrambled to my feet.

"Don't you like snow?" Portia said innocently. "How about this then? Storm at SEA!" She clapped again.

The white mountain vanished. The snow melted and disappeared down little plugholes in the floor.

Lurching waves flashed on to the walls and wind blasted from all directions. It really felt like we were on a boat. I staggered. Was the floor actually tilting?

Lightning crackled from the ceiling right over my head. Distracted, I missed Wendy's next move. She struck my arm and I toppled over.

"Stand back and I'll turn Wendy off," Rufus yelled over the noise of the storm. "Don't panic, Robyn. We train like this every day so we know what to do."

"No!" I scrambled up again, gritting my teeth. I wasn't going to back away – I was going to beat this Wendy machine and then the BUTT kids would see I wasn't panicking. The more I dodged, the more I could see a pattern in Wendy's strikes. I was pretty sure I could tell where her next move would be.

I feinted left. Then thrust to the right, slashing her red shirtsleeve, but my sword bounced off her arm. Shifting back, I dodged her return blow. This was gonna be tough. I had to strike harder.

I locked eyes with Wendy. Voices buzzed around me but I took no notice. Any second now, I'd get my chance.

I dived under her guard, sweeping my frostblade

in a wide arc. Her arm cracked open and a mass of metal bolts cascaded to the floor.

"Robyn, wait!" Aiden called.

But I couldn't stop. I was close to victory – I could see it in Wendy's glassy green eyes. I struck her shoulder and she fell, hitting the ground at an awkward angle. A panel snapped open in her back and wires sparked.

"Warning!" Wendy croaked. "System meltdown."

Rufus clapped his hands, yelling, "Weather off!"

The wind dropped and the image of heaving waves disappeared from the walls. I stepped closer, pushing my hair out of my eyes. My stomach did a somersault. Had I really beaten her?

The robot's eyes rolled and her arms and legs twitched. More bits of metal and plastic fell out of the crack in her arm. Then she lay still.

I grinned and turned to the others. "Did you see that? I won!"

Tristan looked furious and Portia had gone bright red. I didn't care about the BUTT kids, but I was surprised that Aiden looked angry too. "Robyn, are you crazy?" He knelt down beside the robot, shooting me an accusing look. "Why did you do that? Now you've broken Wendy."

We Meet the Trofflegurt

iden pulled at the wire poking out of the control panel on Wendy's back. "You couldn't just wait for someone to switch her off, could you? I told you to stop. I knew you'd end up doing something like this."

"I was defending myself," I protested. "Wendy started it when she hurt Nora. Anyway, I didn't mean to break her . . . I just wanted to win."

"You always want to win – that's all you think about!" Aiden took a screwdriver out of his pocket and tried to undo another panel. "I wanted to see how she worked. Not much chance of that now."

"Sorry!" I started to see why Aiden was annoyed. I should have remembered how much he liked mucking about with machines before I struck Wendy so hard. "Maybe she can be fixed."

"I think we should go and tell Mr Dray," Tristan said coldly.

"We don't grass people up, Tristan," Rufus told him. "If the trofflegurt can fix Wendy then Dray doesn't have to know. All we need to do is track it down and let it do its thing."

"I'll fetch it." Portia sped from the hall.

"What's a . . . what did you call it?" Nora asked.

Rufus puffed his chest out. "A trofflegurt. It's been living here for years – I think it's one of a kind."

Portia came back, holding the door open for a stubby creature with long grey hair all over its body. Two horns jutted from its head and every few seconds an electric-blue bolt crackled between them. It was dragging a bulging sack along the floor like some tiny, hairy Santa Claus.

I stared. You could hardly see its feet under all that hair. "You're keeping a creature of the Unseen World as a pet? Isn't that against Federation rules?"

"It's more of a servant than a pet," Tristan corrected me.

The trofflegurt made straight for the damaged

robot. It began tossing things out of its sack – screwdrivers, pins, rolls of tape – and burbling all the while in a funny sing-song voice, although I couldn't understand any of the words. It had little black fingers – maybe a dozen on each hand – and it plucked at the wires poking out of Wendy's body. In seconds, it had neatened them up and tucked them back inside the machine.

"I get it!" Nora said suddenly. "This is how you have so many great gadgets, isn't it? Your watches, the subthermal scanners, the ultrasonic blades – everything was made by this creature."

Rufus fiddled with his watch. "Sometimes we draw designs and that means it's still our ideas. . ."

"You had the idea for an ultrasonic blade?" I asked.

"Well, not that one." Rufus looked awkward.

The trofflegurt stopped burbling and stared round, its black eyes just about visible behind its curtain of hair. Then it carried on pulling things out of the sack until spanners, wire and drawing pins were rolling all over the place. Its sing-song noises grew sharper and the bolt crackled fiercely between its horns.

"We should go," Rufus said. "It gets stressed with too many people around."

"Someone has to stay and keep an eye on it." Portia's mouth twisted. "I think it should be Robyn – she's the one that broke Wendy."

I shrugged. Aiden still looked cross and I was fed up of the BUTT kids already. "Fine, I'll stay. Just come and get me when it's time for dinner." I stretched out on the floor while the others headed off with Rufus and Tristan arguing over whether to take them to Mock Up Street or to some laser acrobatic thing.

I watched the trofflegurt for a while. It shuffled round the collapsed robot, opening panels and moving wires. Every now and then, it stared at me from under its thick grey hair and made a *Rrrr* noise. I looked at my watch and my stomach rumbled. I was sure I could smell pepperoni pizza. What if they'd started dinner but forgotten to come and get me?

The trofflegurt looked fine so I left the combat studio and headed back to where Cryptorum had left us. There was no one around and no sign of dinner. Maybe I could find the kitchen and see how long it was going to be. I followed the smell of baking pizza along the corridor. The passageway curved round in a spiral, sloping downwards all the time. I tried different doors, finding a workshop and a creepy cupboard full of half-finished metal heads. Maybe Wendy wasn't the only robot the trofflegurt had tried to make. I was surprised the BUTT kids had never mentioned the creature before.

The next door opened on to a metal staircase over a deep drop. I flicked on the lights and went to the railing, my footsteps echoing around the huge emptiness. Way, way down was a network of roads, with rows of houses and trees and paths. This must be Mock Up Street – the fake town that Dominic Dray had in his basement. It was HUGE – almost the size of a real town. I hurried out again. It was probably really handy for training but the empty town gave me the shivers.

I reached the back door. Nora, Aiden and the others were outside practising with the ultrasonic blades. I nearly went out there but the smell of pizza was still drifting down the passage. The kitchen must be here somewhere.

I worked my way back, checking every room. I'd nearly given up on finding any food, when I heard soft growling. Pudding was crouched in the entrance hall, hackles up, eyes fixed on something inside one of the rooms.

"Hey, Pudding! What's the matter?" As I got

closer, I saw Storm, the BUTT kids' Chime wolf, standing in the doorway. The white-haired wolf snarled, ready to spring. "Hey, that's enough!" I got between them.

Pudding licked my hand and sat back on his haunches but Storm didn't move an inch. The room he seemed to be guarding was just a study, with a desk and some bookcases. I took a step closer and he gave a fierce growl. Why was he guarding the place? Was there something in there that Dray didn't want anyone to find?

I knelt down, whispering in Pudding's ear. "I need your help, Pudding. I've got to get into that room."

Pudding gave a soft bark. He was a pretty intelligent wolf. He scampered up the passageway, leaping up to pull coats off the coat pegs. Then he snatched Dray's cane, which was leaning up against the wall, and ran off with it. Storm broke into a frenzy of barking and chased after him.

"Go, Pudding!" I dashed into the study and closed the door. "A classic distraction move."

The room looked like any other study, though it was a lot smaller than Cryptorum's. There was a desk in the middle and bookshelves round the walls. I started searching the desk drawers and found a nearly full bag of toffees. That cheered me up straight away. Dray wasn't likely to miss a few. Then I rummaged through the books and bits of paper in the lower drawers. There was nothing that was even a teeny bit interesting – just a book called *How to Talk Your Way to the Top* and some pencil sketches of Mock Up Street. I shut the drawer super quietly and started searching the rest of the room.

Lying on the windowsill was a pile of envelopes weighed down with a snow globe. My stomach turned over as I spotted a Prague postmark on the top envelope. That was where the International Federation of Chimes had their headquarters. I pulled out the letter and noticed it was signed by Mr Fettle – the Federation man who'd come to Grimdean House. I starting reading:

Dear Dominic,

Thank you for contacting me with information about the dream leeches. I am pleased you offered to keep a close eye on matters at Grimdean House. It's not clear to me yet whether the item we talked of will be essential. . .

I stopped, hearing voices in the hall. Stuffing the letter into my pocket, I struggled with the window catch. Sliding the window open, I climbed on to the sill and swung my legs through, before dropping into a bush below. As I crouched there, my mind was spinning. Why had Dominic Dray written to the Federation man about the dream leeches? The part about keeping an eye on what we were doing at Grimdean made my stomach churn. Trust Dray to pretend to be friends while acting like a spy. Should I find Cryptorum and tell him right now?

The door creaked and there were footsteps inside the study. I froze. Branches were scraping my neck, but I didn't dare move.

"I bet she was trying to find the kitchen." Nora's voice floated through the open window. "She probably smelt the pizza and got hungry."

"OK let's look in there," Rufus replied. "I told Mr Dray we'd all stay together. If she went down to Mock Up Street she could get lost for a really long time. . ."

Their footsteps grew quieter as if they were walking away again. I was about to move when someone else spoke.

"Have you asked them about the sword like Dray told us to?" Tristan said.

"I tried talking to Aiden but he was too busy messing around with the ultrasonic blades," Portia replied. "I'm not asking the midget. She'll figure out why we want to know too quickly."

I tensed, listening really carefully. What did they mean – ask about which sword?

"You should ask Robyn when we find her. She'll never work it out." They laughed and their footsteps got quieter.

I waited a couple of minutes before climbing out of the bush. Then I made my way round the side of the house. Aiden, Nora and Rufus were trying to separate Pudding and Storm as they snapped and snarled at each other.

"You'd think Chime wolves would have some sense of fellowship," Nora puffed, trying to hold Pudding back. "Oh, Robyn! Give me a hand."

"Do you call that thing a Chime wolf?" Portia, who'd just emerged from the house with Tristan, looked mockingly at Pudding. "Chime wolves have white coats and green eyes, and they're strong and brilliant at tracking monsters. That's just a *dog*."

My insides boiled. "Pudding is not a dog – he's a Chime wolf! He's been trained to find monsters and he can do anything Storm can do."

"Hey, don't start!" Rufus tried to stand between me and Portia but she pushed him out of the way.

"Are you really stupid enough to believe that?

Or maybe you're just lying. You can see by looking at him that's he's just an ordinary mutt." She smirked.

"A bit of an ugly one actually," Tristan added.

Pudding leapt on Tristan, knocking him over. He planted his front paws on Tristan's chest and growled.

"He's a pretty intelligent wolf actually. That's how he knows you're an idiot." I clicked my fingers. "Pudding, come here! I'm going back to the car. I wouldn't eat your dinner if it was the last pepperoni pizza on Earth."

Pudding Goes on the Hunt

knew Miss Smiting was on my side about arguing with the BUTT kids because she picked up a takeaway pizza for me on the way back to Wendleton. Cryptorum was in a grump though. "You have to learn to control your temper, Robyn." He turned stormy grey eyes on me. "You can't let people provoke you like that."

That was hilarious – he let people provoke him all the time! Pointing it out wasn't going to help though. "They were mean about Pudding! At least I found out something useful – there was a letter from that Federation man in Mr Dray's study." I delved into my pocket but the letter was gone. I checked around the back seat. "Bother! It must have fallen out of my pocket back at Kesterly Manor."

"What did it say?" Nora asked.

I screwed up my forehead. "Um . . . I only read the first bit before I had to hide. It thanked Dray for spying on us and it said something about the dream leeches. . ."

"You shouldn't have gone snooping through Mr Dray's things," Cryptorum growled. "Honestly, Robyn, if you're trying to wreck everything you're going the right way about it."

"I was trying to help!" I said, stung. "It proves that Dray's spying on us and telling the Federation what we do. Aren't you worried about that?"

"Of course he's telling them!" Cryptorum replied. "I know what kind of man he is. But we need him right now and that's all there is to it."

I gaped. Cryptorum knew that Dray was reporting what we did to the Federation and he still wanted to be friends with him!

"Mr Dray was really nice today – he gave me one of his special watches." Aiden pushed up his sleeve and admired a sleek black watch just like the ones the BUTT kids wore. "And I've got so many ideas for new inventions now I've seen more of their gadgets."

"You shouldn't wear that," I said. "Dray could be using it to spy on us right now!"

"Don't be silly! There's no camera or microphone – I'd be able to tell if there was." Aiden turned away from me.

I had to convince everyone to be more careful about Dominic Dray. I remembered what I'd overheard Tristan saying to Portia – how they'd wanted to ask about a sword. "I know Dray's up to something because of what I heard Portia and Tristan say—"

"That's enough, Robyn," Cryptorum interrupted me. "We're all tired and it doesn't do any good to go on about things."

I sank back into the limo seat, arms folded. So none of them wanted to listen to me. Well, that was fine! But I wouldn't let Dominic Dray stitch us up if I could help it.

Black clouds hung low over Grimdean House all week and the bats seemed restless. They came out in the daytime, buzzing round the Grimdean tower and the weapons shed as if they were guarding the place. Cryptorum disappeared most days and Miss Smiting said he was using the DED machine to look for trails of dark energy.

With Cryptorum absent, Pudding was free to trot around Grimdean House during school time. His best trick was to hide under the dining tables at lunch and let all the kids feed him chips. On Thursday, he came into the grand parlour where the whole school was gathered for assembly and sat down right next to me. The whole of my row began to giggle and the people in front of us turned round to see what was going on. Mrs Lovell hadn't noticed though as she was asking Mrs Perez to play a song for us on the piano. The opening bars of "All Things Bright and Beautiful" rang out and Pudding's ears pricked up.

"Stay low, Pudding," I muttered, but the Chime wolf obviously had no intention of hiding. He wagged his tail as we started singing and each time we got to the end of a line, he barked loudly.

"All things bright and beautiful. . ." (Woof!)

"All creatures great and small. . ." (Woof woof!)

The whole room burst out laughing. Mrs Lovell fiddled with her necklace, her face growing pink. "Robyn Silver! Please take that dog out at once. He really shouldn't be downstairs during school hours."

I hugged Pudding as soon as we got outside. "You got me out of assembly. Good boy!"

The bell went for break time so I decided to sneak upstairs and see if Cryptorum was there, even though I wasn't supposed to go up till after school. I'd thought a lot about what I'd overheard at Kesterly Manor and knew I had to explain it to him. Tristan had said that Dray was making them ask us about a sword and if Dray wanted to know then it had to be important.

I waited till everyone had run outside, then I checked the corridor for teachers before calling Pudding to follow me. When I reached the top, I found Aiden had got to the study before me. The black DED machine was on the desk and Cryptorum was fiddling with the dials.

"We should definitely get our own trofflegurt," Aiden was saying. "I could make so many new things with a trofflegurt to help me. I could make a much better version of that machine. It's quite old, isn't it?"

Cryptorum's eyebrows twitched the way they always did when he was irritated. "This machine works fine. And no you can't have a trofflegurt. They're exceedingly rare and in any case we probably have enough hamlings around the place to fill our quota of monster pets. Not to mention Eye!"

Eye, who had been sunning herself on the windowsill, scuttled behind the curtains as soon as her name was mentioned. Pudding trotted over to sniff the little crab.

"What are hamlings?" I began, but a high-pitched squeal from the DED interrupted me.

"There's something close ... very close!" Cryptorum muttered and, grabbing the machine with one hand and his coat with the other, he dashed out of the door.

I longed to follow him but the bell rang for the end of break. Aiden and me were left to plod downstairs and go back to lessons.

When I came upstairs at the end of school, Nora was reading in the armchair and Aiden was by the window.

"I guess Cryptorum's still out then?" I crouched down to rub Pudding's fur. I remembered my question from earlier. "Hey – what are hamlings? Cryptorum mentioned them and I've never heard of them before."

Nora looked up from her book. "They're like little silver mice with big oval ears and they like to collect things – small things like pens and keys – which they carry away to their nests. There might be a picture in here." She started leafing through the pages.

"At least with Cryptorum out, we'll have lots of time to train Pudding." I patted my leg. "Ready, Pudding? Here boy!"

"Actually, I think I'll spend some time in the workshop." Aiden headed out of the door. "I'll see you later."

I frowned as I looked for the key to the weapons shed in Cryptorum's desk. I'd thought Aiden would be excited about training Pudding with me. "Is he still mad at me about breaking Wendy?" I asked Nora.

"I don't know." Nora put the book down and picked up her torchblade. "I reckon he wanted to spend longer at Kesterly and … not leave so quickly."

"Oh!" Pudding started scratching at the door. "Come on then. I think Pudding wants us to get a move on."

The Chime wolf galloped up and down the lawn like a puppy as soon as we got outside. Nora found a tennis ball left by the hedge and we threw it for him to fetch. Pudding hurtled across the garden, knocking into Obediah's wheelbarrow and sending it flying.

"Hey, Pudding, slow down!" I picked up the chewed-in-half ball and threw it all the way across the lawn. Then I went to unlock the weapons shed. "It's a shame we can't go out monster hunting. We could train Pudding much better if we weren't stuck in here."

"Cryptorum would be furious if we went monster hunting without his permission. We could hide things around the garden and get Pudding to track them down," Nora suggested. "I was reading about Chime wolves last night and they have ten times better hearing and smell than a normal wolf."

Feeling around, I discovered the edges of the trapdoor hidden under a mat. This was what I'd been looking for – the hatch Cryptorum had opened to bring out the Dark Energy Detector the other night. I tried the key but it wouldn't fit in the lock. I stood up and dusted off my hands. Maybe there was something I could use to prise the hatch open...

Pudding galloped over with the ball and dropped it at my feet. Then he sniffed at the hatch and growled.

"What are you doing?" Nora stared. "I thought we were going to train Pudding."

"Cryptorum's storing things down there and I want to know what they are. There could be loads of interesting weapons." I glanced round the shed. Cryptorum's best sword, the one with the swirly markings, had vanished. Was he storing that below where I couldn't reach it?

"Come *on*!" Nora folded her arms. "I have to go home in half an hour – my parents get annoyed if I'm late."

The Mortal Clock on the Grimdean tower started chiming, as if to prove that I was wasting time.

"Sorry!" I closed the shed. It wasn't very often that Nora got impatient and if Cryptorum had the key to the trapdoor there wasn't much I could do right now. "OK, what shall we hide for Pudding?" I scanned the garden. "Where *is* Pudding?" I spotted the wolf, crouched in front of the fir trees at the bottom of the garden, still as stone.

"Something's happened!" Nora started running and I sprinted after her.

Pudding's ears were pricked high and his tail pointed straight out behind him. His lips were drawn back from his teeth in a silent snarl.

"What is it, Pudding?" I scanned the trees. "Is it a monster?"

Pudding gave a short bark. Tensing, he galloped between the fir trees and leapt straight over the high fence behind them.

"Pudding!" Nora gasped. "I can't believe he jumped that. It's six foot high."

I started climbing the nearest tree, pine needles scratching my face. "We've gotta go after him. He's alone out there."

"But we're not supposed to leave the ... oh, there's no point in arguing with you, is there?" Nora sighed.

"Nope!" I climbed higher and a branch cracked under my feet and gave way. I was left kicking in mid-air as I clung desperately to the tree trunk.

"Robyn, stop mucking around." Nora's voice came from the other side of the garden. "Obediah's unlocked the back gate for us."

I dropped from the tree, scrambled up from the dirt and raced over. A smile spread over Obediah's wrinkled face as he held the gate open for us. "Don't be too long, my ducks. It'll be dark soon."

I sprinted through. "Thanks, Obediah!" It wasn't the dark that worried me. It was how mad Cryptorum would be if he found out we'd left Grimdean House without permission. Stepping into the street, I scanned right and left. "Pudding?"

Somewhere to the left there was a distant growl. We followed the sound, passing a row of neat houses. We saw no one and that struck me as weird. Usually there'd be kids playing out after school.

The street was a dead end with a fence at the bottom. Somewhere out of sight, Pudding broke into a torrent of barking that ended in a whine. Pushing my way through a hole in the fence, I found myself on a football field with a playground on one side. I remembered coming here once with Mum and Annie but I didn't know the place very well. Pudding was crouched by the slide, his ears flat against his head, staring at a dark, shifting shape behind the climbing frame.

"He *has* found something." Nora twisted her plait nervously. "Shall we go back and tell Cryptorum?"

"No way! This is our first hunt with a Chime wolf. Let's see what Pudding's found." I started running through which monsters it could be in my head. The dark shape looked bigger than a kobold but smaller than a grodder. It wasn't likely to be a boggun as they rarely showed themselves and it couldn't be a vodanoy as there wasn't any water close by.

I caught a flash of white and for a second I was sure it was a scree sag. Then the figure straightened and I saw the whiteness was the back of a man's neck. I crept a bit closer. The man had short dark hair and long delicate hands that reminded me of the time my finger got stretched by the DED machine. The darkness round the edge of the playground thickened and Pudding snarled softly.

"It's just a man, isn't it?" I whispered to Nora

She shivered. "I don't know. Why is he just standing there?"

I crept closer still. The man seemed motionless but it was hard to see in the dim light. I hesitated. The last thing I wanted to do was whip out a frostblade right in front of an ordinary person who'd probably phone the police. Pudding growled again and the man half-turned, lifting one long hand as if to silence the wolf. His dark coat seemed to ripple.

"Don't mind Pudding — we're still training him," I called out. "So ... um ... sorry about all the growling." My hand moved to rest on the torchblade in my pocket. Why didn't this guy reply? Why wasn't he even looking at us?

"Let's go," Nora whispered.

Something ran over my foot – it was a dream leech crawling over the toe of my shoe. I shook it off just as a car came round a bend in the nearby road, its headlights sweeping over the park for a few seconds.

In that instant I saw things I never want to see again. There were dream leeches everywhere – scuttling over the grass, covering the slide and swings. The man behind the climbing frame had blank eyes like empty white holes and his mouth was a cavern of grinning shark teeth.

Just looking at him froze my insides. This was a monster, not a man. No wonder I'd thought he could be a scree sag – his skin was ghost-white. The movement on his coat wasn't the material rippling but dream leeches swarming all over him. His awful smile glinted in the last flash of light from the passing car. Then darkness dropped over the playground again.

I pulled the torch out of my pocket and my finger hovered over the frostblade button. Blood thumped in my ears. "Get back! Nora. . ." No sound was coming out of my mouth. I tried again. "Nora. . ." My voice wasn't working.

I could see Nora's lips moving too but neither of us made a sound. I managed to swallow but my tongue felt thick and wrong. Had the monster stolen our voices? Smart monster move – it meant we couldn't shout for help any more. . .

Pudding turned tail and ran, and me and Nora raced after him. All I could think about was getting away from that playground. Halfway across the playing field, I collided with a group of bigger kids, bouncing off a boy who was wearing his school tie as a bandana.

"For goodness' sake, Robyn!" Sammie emerged from behind the lanky teenager, a bag of open gummy sweets in her hand. "Stop running round like an idiot. It's so embarrassing being related to you."

How could I warn them about the monster when I had no voice? I took a really deep breath. "It's not safe!" I shouted, then broke off. My voice was working again.

"Jeez, Robyn! Stop shouting." Sammie breezed past me. "And why do you have to carry that torch around all the time? It isn't even properly dark yet. Think you're on some kind of adventure, don't you?" Her gang walked on, laughing.

"She's right, it isn't dark. But it was before – I know it was." Nora's face was pinched and pale. "What *was* that thing? Those horrible white eyes. . ."

128

I stared back at the playground on the other side of the field. The darkness had lifted somehow. The sun had set but the last shreds of daylight were glinting off the metal chains that held the swings. The space behind the climbing frame was empty. "It's disappeared – whatever it was. We have to tell Cryptorum about this."

Nora shivered. "I hope he doesn't want help finding it – I just want to go home. We're going to be in so much trouble for leaving the garden."

I shrugged. "He's always mad with me about something." I didn't want to admit it but I'd much rather face an angry Cryptorum than see that creepy monster again.

10

Miss Smiting Remembers an Old Tale

y breath thudded in my chest as we ran back along the road to Grimdean. Obediah had locked the back gate so we had to go all the way round the front to get in. Miss Smiting appeared in the entrance just as we ran up the steps – she seemed to have a sixth sense for when there was trouble.

"What iss it?" She scanned our flushed faces. "Tell me quickly."

I swallowed. My throat still felt strange. "Pudding found a monster – something we've never seen before."

Miss Smiting ordered Pudding to stay before leading us into the secret passage that ran inside the Grimdean walls. We hurried down the narrow corridor, passing rooms on either side that were only visible through tiny peep holes, until we reached stone steps that took us down to the basement. Three doors stood between us and the dungeon. The first time I'd been here I'd thought having three doors in a row was stupid. That was before I discovered what was locked inside.

Cryptorum was kneeling on the stone floor, trying to pull a scree sag out of a sack. The monster had fastened its long bony fingers on to the material and wouldn't be shaken off. Cryptorum sighed and thrust the whole sack entangled with the monster into an open cage before banging the door shut. "That's another one gone," he said grumpily. "They're starting to ask me at the DIY store why I buy so many sacks."

The kobold in the cage next door began to growl, its spines bristling. "Quiet, you!" Cryptorum rapped on the bars.

"Quiet, you!" snarled an identical voice from a cage in the corner.

"A mimicus!" Nora edged closer to the large transparent blob, staring in fascination. An eye on a stalk sprang out of the monster's body and stared right back.

"That's just wrong!" I shuddered as the horrible eye swivelled round. Then, with a popping-squelching sound, three more eyes sprang out of the creature's jelly-like body and twisted in my direction.

"I've read about mimicuses but I thought they were rare," Nora said.

"These days everything I catch is rare." Cryptorum flicked a row of switches, lighting up the far end of the huge dungeon, and my stomach swooped as I saw that each cage had a monster that looked creepier than the last.

There was a tall, one-legged creature with fangs, jumping up and down like a pogo stick. In the cage next door, there was a huge black dog with three eyes. Beyond that, a flock of little birds with red and gold feathers circled the largest pen and I wondered why Cryptorum had captured ordinary budgies until the birds flew together and morphed into a giant winged thing with enormous talons and a squawk that shook the dungeon. It was a neat trick and I would have been more impressed if the horrible image of the monster at the playground hadn't been burned into my brain.

"Erasmuss, the children saw a new kind of monster outside," Miss Smiting told him. "I will find Aiden and bring him down here. It iss high time we all had a proper talk."

Cryptorum sighed as Miss Smiting swept out the door. He obviously wasn't in a talking mood. "Well then, what was it? Surely no monsters got into my garden?"

I started telling him what happened. His eyebrows bristled more fiercely than the kobold's spines when I reached the bit about leaving the Grimdean grounds. "So it was definitely something we haven't seen before," I said hurriedly, hoping he would focus on that and not on how we'd run out of Grimdean alone in pursuit of a monster. "It had white eyes and really pointed teeth and when we couldn't speak – that was the scariest bit. It was as if the monster had stolen our voices. . ."

"What do you mean? That didn't happen!" Nora stared. "I could hear you yelling the whole time – I was worried people would hear you actually! It was when we shrank down to half our normal size that it got really frightening. I felt so small and when I ran I hardly moved a millimetre!"

It was my turn to stare. We didn't shrink! Why was Nora saying that?

Cryptorum had turned his attention to a large

wooden crate with blackened edges. "If you can't even agree on what happened, how do you expect me to believe you? You probably saw some poor chap who just wanted to smoke a pipe in peace. So what if he had an odd-looking face?"

I rolled my eyes. Smoke a pipe! What century did he think we were living in? "His eyes had no pupils. They were just blank white circles! This was definitely a monster – a really bad one."

"Well, that narrows it down." Cryptorum crouched beside the crate.

"This is serious! It WAS a monster." My voice rose. "And we need to get back out there and catch it before it hurts somebody."

Cryptorum shot me a look. "What *exactly* was it about to do? Could it grab people with its long tentacles or trample them with its enormous hooves?"

"Er . . . well it was staring in a really horrible way and . . . well I could just tell that it was dangerous. Even Pudding was scared."

Cryptorum turned back to the crate. "So you want me to hurry out to find this monster or person that wasn't threatening anyone at all? Forgive me if I don't rush for my sword. Now be quiet a minute – I need to concentrate." He drew out a screwdriver and jiggled it in the crate's lock while trying to stay at arm's length.

"What's in there?" I interrupted, just as flames burst through the wooden slats of the box.

Cryptorum jerked back, cursing. "For goodness' sake! Can't you keep quiet for a second, Robyn?"

"Sorry!" Another flame burst through the slats – fiery orange with a tinge of blue at the tip. The box caught alight and tiny flames licked around the edges. Nora squeaked and jumped back.

"Dratted thing! It'll turn the whole box to ash." Cryptorum plunged in and sprang the lock open. "Stand back, everyone."

A creature with deep purple skin, like a lion crossed with a dragon, sprang from the crate. Its tail twitched from side to side and the ring of red spikes around its neck bristled. It looked awesome in a deadly kind of way. Smoke filled the room as the edges of the box continued to smoulder.

"Don't go near the tail!" Cryptorum grabbed a spare sack and threw it over the monster, who thrashed violently.

I snatched up another sack and rushed to help. "Why? Does it have spikes or something?"

"What's that?" Cryptorum wrestled with the sack-covered creature.

"The tail – why is it dangerous?" I clutched one of the monster's legs but it shot out of my grasp and hurtled round the dungeon. Fire burst out of the end of its tail, spraying the cages and setting the other monsters screeching and yowling. "Woah! OK, so *that's* why."

The creature tore round the room, climbing the sides of cages and galloping across the ceiling. It stopped halfway and gave a deafeningly triumphant roar, which set all the other monsters off for a second time. The kobold snarled while the scree sag rattled the bars of its cage with its bony white fingers. The pogo stick with fangs bounced like crazy and the giant bird in the corner divided into masses of little birds that flew in circles so fast it made me dizzy.

Cryptorum hit a big black button on the wall and an alarm bell rang. "Robyn, stop daydreaming and give me a hand!" He was struggling with a ball of blue netting so I grabbed one end and Nora ran to help too. Together we swung it through the air just as the beast leapt over the next cage. The creature landed, struggling, in the net. Fire blasted everywhere and I dropped the blue mesh and dived behind a crate, dragging Nora with me.

Miss Smiting swept through the door and

emptied a bucket of water all over the creature. Smoke rose and the fire beast spluttered. Cryptorum dragged it into a spare cage and slammed the door shut.

"Quick, Aiden – the other bucket!" ordered Miss Smiting, and Aiden rushed in and poured water over the burning sacks and wooden crate. The fire fizzled out and the room filled with a sour burnt smell. Miss Smiting glided over to the big black button on the wall and stopped the alarm before checking each of the cages were secure.

"What IS that creature?" I demanded.

"A crike. It's rare even in deserts where it likes to live and it shouldn't be here at all." Cryptorum rubbed his soot-stained face. There was a tuft of smoking hair at the top of his forehead. "I found it playing in a sandpit on Compton Road. Goodness knows what I'm going to do with it."

The crike sulkily turned its back and started washing its paws with a purple tongue. Now it had stopped leaping around and squirting fire from its tail, it looked like an odd purple-ish leopard. It was definitely the strangest monster I'd seen – and I'd seen some really weird things lately.

Cryptorum leaned against the kobold's cage, puffed out. "I'm exhausted," he said to Miss

Smiting. "I've caught so many creatures lately that I'm running out of cages down here. All these rare monsters suddenly showing up has to mean something is drawing them here. Something big. . ." He swept a sooty hand through his mane of grey hair. "And that means whatever's coming could appear very soon. Then – just to make things even harder – I've got these three ninnies roaming the place with that giant dog and drawing lots of attention to themselves."

"I've been inside the whole time," Aiden said. "I was working on my monster radar upstairs."

Cryptorum lifted one eyebrow. "Well at least one of you has some sense."

My face burned. "We didn't draw attention to ourselves! We're not that stupid." I decided to leave out the part where we ran into Sammie and her friends. "And Pudding is a Chime wolf not a dog. And the thing we saw really was a monster – I just know it. You've always told us to trust our instincts – you said they were more useful to us than any gadgets." Aiden frowned at me but I carried on. "I think this is a really bad monster and you should listen to us. So what if our stories don't match up? The monster was THERE and we both saw it!"

Cryptorum sighed. "You saw something in the

twilight and you panicked. That's why you couldn't speak and Nora felt small."

"You're wrong! And we're just wasting time." I turned to Miss Smiting for support. "I know what I saw and if none of you will help I'll find the creature on my own."

"Robyn, don't!" Nora bit her lip.

"I have to!" I insisted. "This could be the dangerous monster that the Federation man warned us about."

"What iss thiss about your stories not matching?" Miss Smiting asked. "Sstart at the beginning and explain."

So I explained it again and described how I'd lost my voice. Nora told them how she'd suddenly found herself half her normal size. Listening to it all, I'd have laughed if I didn't remember how terrified I'd been. Why did we remember it so differently?

"But of course! It all comess back to me now." Miss Smiting started gliding up and down the dungeon, her long skirt swishing. "In the rainforest where I came from there were stories about Awud – the Nightmare Man. It was a tale told around the fire late at night. People said he arrived at dusk as the parrots were roosting and the monkeys returning from gathering fruit. He would slip between the trees, sspreading darkness everywhere he went, and all the people who met him became filled with terrible fears and foreboding. One believed that all his teeth had fallen out, another believed that she was being attacked by a swarm of rats, a third believed he could no longer move a ssingle step." Her green eyes narrowed. "And the longer you spent with the Nightmare Man, the greater the chance that your darkest dream would come true – at least that'ss how the tale went."

"That's why he was covered with dream leeches! They must like him because he's a monster of nightmares ... and I guess when I lost my voice none of that was real." I shifted uncomfortably. It had definitely felt real.

"The book I'm reading has an old tale about the Mara – a monster that controls nightmares," Nora said. "It must be the same monster under a different name."

"I've never heard of it before," Cryptorum grunted. "But it would explain why there have been so many dream leeches in the area." He picked up his frostblade from where it was leaning against the wall. "Show me where you saw this thing."

We locked the dungeon and left Grimdean through the back gate, waiting while Cryptorum fetched the Dark Energy Detector from the shed. Hurrying through the dark, we climbed through the gap in the fence into the empty park. It was pitch-black and I couldn't hold back a shiver as we drew closer to the climbing frame. But this time nothing appeared in the torch beam. There were no dream leeches either. Could the nightmare monster turn invisible or had it gone to another park to terrify some other poor kids? I reminded myself that they wouldn't be able to see it unless they'd been born on the stroke of midnight. Lucky them.

Cryptorum switched on the DED and fiddled with the dials. At once, a screeching noise poured out of the machine.

"Sweet heavenss, Erasmus!" Miss Smiting exclaimed. "What is that noise?"

"That is the highest level of dark energy I've ever found." Cryptorum turned the machine off and raked his fingers through his wild, grey hair. "I must tell Dominic about this. We need to find out exactly what this Mara can do and how dangerous it is."

"Mr Dray probably knows it's here already," I

said. "He'd written to the Federation man about the dream leeches. That's what it said in Mr Fettle's reply. I bet he's been keeping the whole thing from us—"

"Quiet, Robyn!" Cryptorum scowled. "I will decide how to handle Mr Dray. Not you."

"Uh-oh!" Nora peered at her watch. "I was meant to be home an hour ago and I promised not to be late this time."

"I'll walk back with you." I turned away from Cryptorum and we headed towards the safety of the brightly lit streets. Neither of us said anything, but we both slowed down a bit once we'd reached the main road. "You'd have thought Cryptorum would be more grateful that we found this Mara monster. It took him long enough to actually believe we'd found something."

Nora gave me a sideways look. "He's under a lot of pressure, I guess. Once Miss Smiting knew of the monster he took it seriously."

I kicked a bramble out of the way. "He never listens properly. He doesn't trust us to go out tracking monsters and he hasn't trained with us for ages. I think we'd be better off monster hunting on our own."

The Clock
Strikes Thirteen

ryptorum scoured the streets of Wendleton for the next three nights trying to find the Mara monster. Each morning, as we arrived for school, he was just returning from a whole night of searching with the DED machine under his arm.

On the third day, I tracked down Nora and Aiden at the end of school and pulled them to one side. "We have to make Cryptorum take us with him tonight. After all, we're the ones who saw the monster." Aiden shook his head. "Well me and Nora did anyway."

"What's going on here?" Mrs Perez, our class teacher, appeared out of nowhere. "I always see you three in a huddle these days. Why are you hanging around here instead of going home?"

A guilty look grew on Nora's face. I knew how she felt. Mrs Perez had that teacher-ish knack for making you feel as if you were doing something wrong. "We're just about to go to Bat Club." The teacher waited, as if she expected a better explanation than that. "We were ... um ... just talking about what nocturnal creatures we might spot out there." This was true – she didn't know I meant creatures like the Mara.

"I see." Mrs Perez studied us as the corridor started to empty. "You seem to be spending an awful lot of time at this club. Perhaps you'd like to do a show and tell in class on what you've learnt."

My stomach lurched. Show and tell with kobolds and hell wurms!

Luckily Mrs Lovell came round the corner and interrupted us. "Oh, there you are! Nora, hurry up, dear – your mum's waiting for you on the steps and she wants you to come straight away."

"But I'm staying for Bat Club," Nora protested.

"Not if you don't have your parents' permission." Mrs Lovell began shepherding her along. "Come on now. Your mum is keen to get going."

Nora cast me a regretful look and went with

the headmistress. I swung my school bag on to my shoulder and followed them to the entrance. I knew Nora's parents didn't like her spending too much time at Bat Club but I hadn't realized things had got this bad.

A black limousine had drawn up outside and Cryptorum climbed the front steps just as Nora and her mum came down. Cryptorum nodded his head and said hello but Mrs Juniper just hurried Nora away.

"Did you see that?" I said to Aiden.

He nodded. "Poor Nora. I guess she's going to find it hard to come to training from now on."

"We'll find a way – we'll train on Saturdays or something." My mind was working furiously as I headed upstairs to Cryptorum's study. We couldn't let Nora's mum break up our monster-fighting team. I was so busy thinking about it that I didn't notice Cryptorum was in a terrible mood until he started pacing up and down the study muttering under his breath.

"Can we come out with you this time?" I asked.

Cryptorum looked at me as if he'd only just noticed I was there. "You'll just slow me down and I'm already having trouble locating places with dark energy. It's as if this Mara creature doesn't want to be found."

Slow him down! He was the one that was old and creaky.

"Maybe I can operate the Dark Energy Detector. That could speed things up," Aiden said eagerly, but Cryptorum just grunted and headed back downstairs.

The following day, me and Nora raced up to Cryptorum's study at the end of school to search for information on the Mara. It had been Nora's idea to hit the books – though she warned me she only had fifteen minutes to spare. If she didn't get home by four her mum would probably come and collect her again. Cryptorum wasn't around and Miss Smiting had told us he'd gone to Kesterly Manor. Aiden was next door in his workshop. Now and then hammering sounded on the other side of the wall.

"It's no good!" Nora put another dusty leather book on top of the ones beside her. She was sitting on the study floor surrounded by a growing pile. "I can't find any mentions of a Nightmare Man or a monster called the Mara. I really thought that one might have something."

"What about that story you were reading?" I put in. "You said there was a nightmare man in that."

Nora pushed her hair away from her eyes. "It's just a story, so there's not much useful information. It doesn't tell us what the Mara does — what it wants."

"Well it doesn't want ice creams at the park and pizza for tea. That's for sure." I squished a bit of paper into a ball and rolled it along the carpet for Eye, who loved a bit of paper football. The little crab skittered after it, kicking it from claw to claw like a professional footballer. I couldn't help giggling, until Pudding decided he wanted to join in and pounced on the ball of paper and ate it. Eye's claws drooped and she sidled away under the armchair.

"Pudding! Eye was having fun with that." I turned back to Nora. "Isn't there somewhere else you can look? Didn't you say Cryptorum kept some books in the dungeon?"

"He keeps those locked away," she sighed. "We'd have to find the keys for all three basement doors and the one for the cabinet he keeps the books in."

"Maybe we won't need this information. Maybe Cryptorum is getting loooads of help and answers from Dominic Dray," I said sarcastically.

Nora's eyes gleamed and she sat up straight, sending the pile of books toppling over her feet. "That's it! Dominic Dray may have books about this monster – after all, he has that huge library." She jumped up, making a second wobbly tower of books collapse. "We have to go there and read everything he's got!"

The door crashed open and Cryptorum swept in like a rain cloud with Miss Smiting right behind him. "Erasmus," she hissed. "Do sslow down and explain what is the matter!"

"It's Dominic," Cryptorum paced over to the window and stared out, his hands gripped tightly behind his back. "I asked what he knew about the Mara. I told him the monster had been sighted here in town and I asked for his advice. He knows more than he's telling and nothing I say will induce him to be open with me. As usual he advances his own interests at the expense of mine." He suddenly noticed me and Nora by the bookcase and he gave me an extra-hard glare. I thought this was a bit harsh considering it was Nora who'd made all the mess.

"There's nothing else for it." He marched to the door. "I'm going to Prague to make the Federation explain everything. I'll fly tonight."

"But what if the Mara returns? And what if that man from the Federation comes back to inspect our training?" I cried, but he was already gone.

"I should get home." Nora quickly loaded books back on to the shelves. "My mum and dad will get really cross if I'm late. Sorry I can't stay. . ."

I helped Nora put back the books and then I stared out of the window for a while after she'd gone. Pudding got up from his doggie bed and sniffed at my hand. "What are we going to do, Pudding? There was a nightmare monster in town and now we can't even find it."

There was a thumping on the stairs. I peeked out and saw Cryptorum disappearing down the steps with a suitcase. Didn't he want to leave us instructions for while he was gone? Were we supposed to carry on looking for the Mara using the DED machine?

"Mr Cryptorum?" I raced after him but by the time I got to the entrance hall the limousine had gone.

I took Pudding outside and threw sticks for him for a while. When we came back in the sun had set and the corridors were full of shadows. Aiden was still hammering upstairs. Realizing I'd left my school bag in Cryptorum's study, I began climbing the steps just as the Mortal Clock on the tower began to chime. The deep sound echoed round the empty mansion as the chimes kept on going.

I checked my watch. It was half past five. Usually the clock only rang once at half past, so why wasn't it stopping? I started counting each one . . . nine, ten, eleven, twelve, *thirteen*.

The chimes stopped and my heart missed a beat.

Aiden burst out of the workshop. "Did the clock just chime thirteen?" "Yeah it did," I said.

"It was definitely thirteen? Where's Cryptorum? We have to tell him."

"He's gone to Prague. He wants to speak to the International Federation of Chimes and he's probably halfway to the airport by now." I opened a window and leaned out to look at the front of the tower. The hands on the huge golden clock were whizzing round in opposite directions and I could hear an awful grinding sound. "Jeez! I think it's broken."

"Let me see!" Aiden leaned out beside me.

The clock hands went on spinning at high speed and people on the street below stopped to watch. At last the grinding noise finished and the hands came to rest pointing at twenty past five. A cluster of bats flew out of the bat barn and circled the tower.

"Cryptorum won't be happy when he finds out it's broken." I pulled the window shut. Both Aiden and me knew how important the Mortal Clock was to Cryptorum. He'd lived in Grimdean House since he was a boy and the clock chiming midnight had woken his Chime powers long ago. Then last year the clock had woken our Chime powers too.

"I'm going to go up there to look at it," Aiden decided. "Maybe it can be easily fixed."

"Do you need any help?"

Aiden was already halfway down the corridor that led to the tower. "It's all right! I can do it."

So I left a note for Miss Smiting explaining what had happened and then I hugged Pudding before heading home. Bats were still swirling round the clock tower as I walked away from Grimdean House and I suddenly wished Cryptorum hadn't gone away. Why had the clock gone wrong so suddenly? I just hoped Aiden would be able to fix it.

We Take Our Monsters on a Day Trip

A iden couldn't fix the Mortal Clock, even though he tried for hours, so the clock hands were stuck permanently at twenty past five. It was odd being at Grimdean without the sound of the chimes – I'd never thought I'd miss it.

Nora was still banned from staying for Bat Club after school so I knocked at her house on Saturday morning and her dad said she could take Pudding for a walk with me. We went to knock on Aiden's door too but his mum told us she'd dropped him off at some gadget festival. Pudding galloped around Penhurst Park and got lots of stares for being the biggest, hairiest animal there. Then I persuaded

Nora that we should go back to my house. I was pretty sure Sammie and Ben would both be out and I knew Mum had bought two packets of choc-chip cookies when she went shopping yesterday.

I sneaked down the side alley and peered through our kitchen window. "It's OK. No one's around." I opened the back door and Pudding bounded inside.

"Are you sure your parents won't mind Pudding being here?" Nora said, doubtfully. "Mine don't like a lot of mess."

I looked at the enormous pile of washing-up in the sink and the breakfast cereal scattered over the table. "Well I think mine have got used to mess." I went to the cupboard and searched at the back behind the flour where I'd seen Mum put the cookies yesterday. Where were they? They couldn't *all* have been eaten already!

"Not looking for these, are you?" Sammie slouched in the doorway, a packet of cookies in her hand. She pulled one from the packet and bit into it slowly, making a loud crunch.

I judged the distance between us. There was no way I'd manage to get the biscuits away from her. She was too fast. "Where's the other packet? There were two."

"Ben took it with him when he went out." Sammie smiled and crunched into another cookie.

I rummaged in the cupboard and pulled out some soggy-looking crackers. I could hear the sound of the TV and Annie and Josh arguing over something.

Mum bustled in. "Robyn, don't eat everything in the cupboard, please. I only went shopping yesterday." Sammie quickly hid the cookie packet behind her back

"I'm not!" I said. "I was just looking for a snack for me and Nora."

"Hi, Nora." Mum smiled and went over to the sink, nearly tripping over Pudding, who'd been concealed from view by the kitchen table. "Oh my goodness! Robyn, where did this enormous dog come from? Please don't tell me you just found him and brought him home."

"He's Mr Cryptorum's. We took him for a walk," I explained. Did Mum really think I'd brought a random dog home?

"Can you take him outside, please?" Mum said. "He's probably got muddy paws."

I sighed and called to Pudding, tucking the crackers into my pocket. Trudging down the garden, I unlocked the shed. "At least it's private in here," I said to Nora. "Has your mum said why she won't let you stay for Bat Club?"

"She had a nightmare about Grimdean House – something about giant spiders with wings." Nora plonked herself on an upside-down bucket beside a pile of broken tennis rackets. "That's why she won't let me stay late. I used to think her biggest nightmare was me not finishing my homework."

"My parents never notice whether I do my homework. It's my brothers and sisters that are always poking their noses in." I ruffled Pudding's fur.

"I keep thinking about the Mara." Nora picked up a tennis racket and fiddled with the strings. "It's annoying that we know so little about it and there are more dream leeches everywhere – I found one crawling right across my window this morning. I think the Mara's behind it all. Maybe he's making more and more leeches and everyone in Wendleton is getting nightmares because of it."

"Maybe." I frowned, remembering Annie calling out in her sleep the night before. Her bad dreams always disturbed me because we shared a room. "But I thought nightmares came from inside people like wishes do."

Pudding pricked up his ears at a scuffling sound

and something flicked past the shed window. I swung the door open. "Annie? Josh?" There was no one there.

Sammie sprang round the shed corner, smirking when I jumped. "Holding a secret meeting of your secret club, dork brain?"

I slammed the door shut. "Go away! This is private!"

"Aww!" She made a face at the window. "I heard you! You're talking about your nightmares, you poor little baby." She headed back towards the house, laughing.

"Dammit!" I watched her through the cobwebby window.

"Just ignore her! We've got to focus on this." Nora started pacing up and down the shed like Cryptorum did around his study. "With Cryptorum away we have to do this ourselves. It's too urgent to wait till he returns. I think we should go over to Kesterly Manor and read everything they've got on the Mara."

I stared at her. Nora didn't usually get worked up like this. "Dray will never let us into his library. He refused to even tell Cryptorum what he knew."

"*Maybe* it doesn't matter whether he lets us." Nora paused before starting to pace again. "Maybe we can set up a diversion! Then no one will realize I'm missing – and I think it *has* to be me. They'll be watching you really carefully after what happened last time you were there but they'll hardly notice I'm gone."

My eyebrows rose. "Are you sure you're feeling OK? You know you'll be in serious trouble if they catch you. What sort of thing do you mean by a diversion anyway?"

Nora smiled. "Ooh, well . . . that's the fun part!"

Two hours later, Miss Smiting drove us through the gates of Kesterly Manor in Obediah Brown's big white van. We'd spent most of the time in between convincing her that Nora's plan was a good idea. This had been tricky as the plan was quite mad – awesome, but mad.

The back of the van was stuffed with monster cages containing the strangest creatures that Cryptorum had captured lately. The crike was grooming its purple fur and ignoring all the other creatures. Me and Nora had wrapped a fire blanket round its tail for safety. Nora had taught me the names of the other rare monsters while we carried the cages upstairs and into the back alley for loading.

The one that looked like a pogo stick with fangs was called a jooper and it broke into bouts of jumping every time we hit a bump in the road. The three-eyed black dog was a gruckle and the giant bird that broke apart into lots of tiny birds was called a multi-winged skitting. I'd remembered the mimicus, of course, and the disgusting way it pushed eyes on stalks out of its jelly-like body. Would a plan involving this many weird monsters really work? It would have been easier with Aiden's help but we'd knocked for him again and he still wasn't home.

"This had better work!" I told Nora for the fiftieth time. She was beside me in the passenger seat. "I can't believe this was your idea. I'm supposed to be the one that does crazy stuff."

Nora grinned. "I promise I've thought it through."

"That's more than I ever do." I checked my pocket for my torchblade again. I wanted the sword handy in case things went wrong.

"We must all sstick to the plan." Miss Smiting cast us a sideways glance. "No – how do you say? – improvisations and making it up as you go along, Robyn, and no losing your temper with those other kidss. You have to be calm AND patient at all timess."

"Calm AND patient!" echoed the mimicus, in a perfect imitation of Miss Smiting's hissing tones.

I grimaced. The thought of seeing Portia's smug face wasn't making me feel very patient.

"Don't act too calm though," Nora added. "It's got to be believable."

My frown deepened. Acting was not my strong point.

We jerked to a stop and Miss Smiting opened the back of the van while we knocked on the front door of the manor. Rain pattered down and we huddled under the porch roof. When the seconds ticked by and no one answered, I started wondering what we'd do if Dominic Dray refused to let us in. Then a bolt scraped back and the door swung open to reveal Tristan's pinched face. "What do you want? Mr Dray's busy."

With a huge effort I held back from telling him exactly what I thought of him. It was hard to decide which of the BUTT kids was the rudest sometimes.

"Hi, Tristan. We're in *such* a mess!" Nora clasped her hands together. "Could you get Mr Dray? We really need his help."

I looked at Nora admiringly. She was pretty convincing. I tried to copy her expression, widening my eyes and making my mouth sort of wobbly. "We just don't know what to do!" I gasped and Tristan frowned suspiciously. I knew I'd be no good at acting.

"Fine! Just wait here and I'll get him." He shut the door again.

I let loose with an eye-roll. "Honestly! He's such an idiot – leaving us out here when it's raining."

"Shh! They'll hear you inside." Nora scooted out the way as Miss Smiting brought the first monster cage up the steps. I went to the van and lifted the jooper's cage, which I reckoned would be lighter than some of the others, but the creature went crazy when it felt raindrops, jerking the cage so much I nearly dropped it. I carried the crike across next but it didn't like the rain either and struck up a high-pitched yowl.

"Well! You're a little far from home, aren't you?" Mr Dray stood at the door with a smile that didn't reach his eyes. Portia and Tristan craned over his shoulder and their mouths dropped open when they saw the mimicus and the jooper.

"Oh, Mr Dray, I'm so glad to see you!" Nora said, earnestly. "We've got all these strange monsters – they're almost spilling out of the dungeon back at

Grimdean House – and with Mr Cryptorum away we just don't know what to do."

Supporting himself on his silver-topped cane, Dray leaned in for a closer look. "Is that a crike? Good gracious, girl! Do you want to set the house on fire?"

"Don't worry, we wrapped up its tail," I began breezily before Nora caught my eye. "Um . . . but it's been totally scary driving over here with all these monsters!"

Miss Smiting set the final cage containing the multi-winged skitting down on the doorstep. "You'd be doing uss such a favour if you looked after these creaturess, Dominic. I told the children you would be sure to help. You have ssuch wonderful facilities here at Kesterly – all the space and the superior technology. What better place to come to!"

While Dray was preening, I carefully swept my hands along the jooper's cage behind me until I found the catch. Then I pulled it open.

"I've worked very hard to make this place what it is," Dray smirked. "So let me take a closer look at these beasts."

"This is the grickle!" Nora told him, deliberately getting it wrong. "It has three eyes as you see and a very nasty growl. . ."

"It's a *gruckle* not a grickle!" Dray laughed and patted Nora on the head. Meanwhile, I edged in front of the skitting's cage and opened that too. "And there's more to worry about than just its growl! It has the strongest jaw of any monster I've ever met. Once it locks on to something it will never let go."

As I moved towards the mimicus's cage, I caught a flicker in Nora's eyes. I got the feeling she knew all that information already. Miss Smiting slipped past the crike's cage and gave a slight nod. We were ready to go.

A shout came from inside. "Portia? I think I've got the alternator working. Come and see!"

I froze. Was that . . . but it couldn't be!

"Portia? Tristan?"

Portia saw my confusion and called back, grinning. "We're over here. We've got some visitors!"

Aiden dashed down the entrance hall and stopped abruptly. He was carrying a metal ball the size of a football with wires sprouting from the top and there was a screwdriver stuck behind his ear. "Oh!" Doubt flashed across his face. "I didn't know you were coming."

A cold feeling washed over me. "You mean you

didn't want us to know you were here. How many times have you come over without telling us?" Nora nudged me but I ignored her.

Aiden scowled. "You're not my keeper, Robyn."

I felt the cage door moving behind me. I wanted to tell Aiden he'd gone over to the enemy camp. I wanted to tell him he was kidding himself if he thought that Dray and the BUTT kids cared about him or his inventions. But there was no time. Operation Infiltrate Kesterly Library was happening right now.

Fur brushed past my leg and the crike leapt up the manor steps, announcing itself with a yowl. Dray dropped his cane and clutched the door frame. Tristan fell back with a gasp.

My heart thudded. Stick to the plan!

Retreating down the steps, I waved my arms, yelling, "Quickly everyone! One of them is loose!"

Nora joined me at the bottom of the steps, shouting, "Whatever you do – don't let it get inside!"

Miss Smiting joined us and together we blocked the crike's path. The multi-winged skitting swooped out of its pen and the gruckle prowled through the loose cage door. Lastly the mimicus oozed on to the steps and slithered over Dray's foot. The monsters looked at the pouring rain and the three of us waving and yelling at the bottom of the steps. Then they turned and ran the opposite way – right through the door into Kesterly Manor.

Kesterly Manor Becomes a Monster Playground

"Stop them!" Dray pointed a shaking finger at the monsters.

Portia dived for the crike but, with a flick of its tail, the creature shook off the fireproof blanket and galloped down the corridor out of sight. The jooper bounced up to the ceiling, smashing the chandelier so that glass rained down in tiny pieces. Portia drew her ultrasonic blade and swiped at the pogo-ing monster, but it flashed its fangs and bolted. The gruckle shook the rain off its black coat, its three eyes fixed on Dray's silver-topped cane. Then, with a snarl, it leapt right over Dray's head, bowling into Tristan and knocking him over.

"Help me!" Tristan squeaked, but the shaggy monster only sniffed his hair before loping down the passageway.

The mimicus, who had squeezed round the door while no one was watching, began copying Tristan. Gaining speed, it slithered away down the corridor, squeaking, "Help me! Help me!"

"Inside, everyone!" I pulled Tristan up and when everyone was inside I slammed the doors shut. "If we keep these closed they can't escape." I glanced at Aiden before looking away. He was frowning as if he knew none of this was accidental.

"What's wrong with you?" Portia stormed at me. "Your cages must be rubbish – breaking open like that. Now we've got to clean up your mess again!"

Dray's eyes were cold. "Enough! Portia fetch my frostblade, please. Tristan, you must release Storm!"

The hallway turned into chaos. Dray shouted orders. Tristan brought in Storm, the BUTT kids' ferocious-looking Chime wolf, which barked uncontrollably when it picked up a jumble of monster scents. The multi-winged skitting began dive-bombing Miss Smiting and Aiden was yelling something that I couldn't hear.

"Look, there's the gruckle!" I bellowed, charging at it and hoping the BUTT kids would follow.

"Stay back!" Portia elbowed past me. "This is our place and we don't need your help."

"Help me! Help me!" The mimicus called in Tristan's squeaky tones, as it disappeared round the corner.

Tristan flushed. "Go on, Storm." He released the Chime wolf. "Hunt!"

The wolf surged along the passageway and Tristan and Portia rushed after it. Mr Dray was waving his cane at the multi-winged skitting. I glanced back to see Nora disappearing through the door to the library. The plan was working so far. I needed to keep them all chasing monsters for as long as possible.

Aiden stuck the metal ball under his arm. "Robyn, what the hell do you think you're doing? I know you didn't bring these monsters here because you need help. This is one of your stupid ideas, isn't it? It's so obvious that it was thought up by you."

This was pretty unfair but I couldn't tell him the truth – not yet, anyway. "Don't be silly! Where's Rufus? Have you seen him?"

"I don't know. He went out somewhere." Aiden ducked as the skitting split into dozens of birds flying at him like little arrows.

"Here!" I pulled him through the nearest door

and we ended up on the steps leading down to Mock Up Street. Bright strip lights shone over the fake streets and an iron staircase led downwards.

A growl echoed in the stillness below. Peering over the railings, I spotted the gruckle crouching behind a fake tree. Tristan was advancing, his ultrasonic blade flickering in the dim light. The three-eyed monster bared its teeth and prepared to spring.

"Jeez! We'd better help him." I sprinted down the steps two at a time. I loathed Tristan but I couldn't just watch while he turned into a monster snack, especially as we'd set the creatures loose in the first place.

Breathless, I stopped at the bottom. "Where are they?"

"Over there!" Aiden raced to the street corner.

Tristan was backed up against a hedge. Swinging his sword like a baseball bat, he lopped off a whole section of the fake bush without hitting the monster at all. The gruckle leapt and fastened its teeth on his sleek leather jacket. "Argh!" he shrieked. "It's got me!"

"Stop moving!" I tried to grab the monster by the scruff of the neck but Tristan was swaying too much. "Just take the jacket off." I pulled his coat zip open, dragged the jacket off him and threw it to the ground with the gruckle still attached. The monster snarled and shook the jacket like a puppy with a slipper. Tristan hid behind the hedge.

"Aw! He's quite cute for a big monster," I said.

The gruckle shook the jacket again before tearing it into little strips.

"Er . . . ferocious but cute!" I pulled a face. "So how are we going to get him back upstairs?"

"Let me try something." Aiden set down the metal ball he was carrying and twisted two of the wires together. There was a crackling – and the ball started to spin. The gruckle stopped shredding Tristan's jacket and growled at the whirling ball. Then gradually its three eyelids began to droop.

"What happens next?" I hissed.

Aiden hushed me. The ball spun faster and faster until the gruckle slumped to the floor, snoring gently. At last, Aiden touched the ball to slow it down. "It needs a few tweaks – I want to make the effect last longer. It only puts a monster to sleep for a few minutes and it doesn't work on every creature yet. . ."

"It's amazing though!" I said, forgetting for a moment that I was cross with Aiden. "How did you think of it?"

Aiden grinned proudly. "I got the idea from the DED, actually, because of the way it finds dark energy by detecting the right frequency. So I've been playing with the frequencies and what they do to monsters. . ."

Tristan recovered his voice. "Wouldn't it have been more intelligent to do your trick at the top?" He jerked his head at the exit door and smiled sourly. "How do you expect to get a thing that size up the stairs?"

I exchanged looks with Aiden. Tristan was right, which was very annoying. "We're going to carry it up. And you're going to help us."

It took ten minutes to get the gruckle up the stairs because Tristan kept stopping, complaining he was tired. The hallway was even more of a disaster area than before. Dray was shouting curses as the crike hurtled around blasting fire from its tail and blackening the wooden walls. Wendy the robot was fighting the jooper, which bounced up and knocked her head off her shoulders. "Mal-func-tion!" she groaned, her head swinging gently by a few wires.

"Hang on, Wendy!" Aiden ran over, pulling his screwdriver from behind his ear.

I looked over at Miss Smiting, who was shutting

the mimicus back inside its cage. She shook her head slightly. So Nora hadn't reappeared. That meant we had to keep everyone busy and away from the library for a bit longer.

Portia let the Chime wolf chase the crike into a cage before slamming it shut. "We're still missing those birds. We'd better check every room." She walked over to the library and pushed the handle.

"No!" I shouted. "I saw it ... going that way, towards your combat studio."

Portia gave me a scornful look. "What are you waiting for then? Are you scared to go and fetch it yourself?"

I gritted my teeth. Calm and patient ... calm AND patient. "I just thought we could catch it together," I managed.

Tristan dropped the sleeping gruckle on the floor and let me drag it over to a cage by myself. He and Portia ran off towards the combat studio and Miss Smiting followed them with an empty cage. Aiden fixed Wendy's neck bolts in place and tightened them with his screwdriver. I glanced sneakily at the library door. Why was Nora taking so long?

Dray was standing beside the gruckle cage with his back to everyone and I noticed him take something out of his pocket, so I sneaked closer. It was a black wristwatch similar to the ones the BUTT kids wore but this one had a larger screen showing a map with a cluster of small, blinking dots. Dray noticed me looking and thrust the watch back in his pocket just as Portia and Tristan reappeared with Miss Smiting, who was carrying the cage containing the skitting.

"We have retrieved all the creatures," Miss Smiting said. "So now perhapss we could discuss arrangements. . ."

There was a loud *beep* from the pocket where Dray had hidden his watch. At the same moment, Portia and Tristan's wrists started beeping too. They both pressed a button on their watches before looking questioningly at Dray.

"That means he's found the place, doesn't it?" began Tristan. "Shouldn't we. . ."

"Not just now." Dray shot a warning look at his trainees, before turning to Miss Smiting and holding out his hand. "It was wonderful to see you again. . ."

"What do you mean: *he's found the place*?" I interrupted. "Who are you talking about?" But Tristan looked away and Dray ignored me.

"You may leave the beasts to us, my dear, and we will deal with them," Dray told Miss Smiting.

"Best that you go now before another disaster strikes. It's funny how disaster seems to follow Robyn around in particular. Perhaps we should set up extra safety measures before allowing her to visit next time."

My stomach swooped. He was just trying to distract me – I was sure of it. "What was that watch alarm for?" I looked at Aiden. "And why didn't *your* watch beep too?"

"I don't know." Aiden tightened the last of Wendy's bolts.

Blood thumped in my head. Couldn't Aiden see that Dray was using him? "Ask him what it is! Can't you see they're not sharing information with us at all?" I swung to face Dray. "I saw the watch in your pocket with the dots on the screen. You're tracking everyone wearing those watches, aren't you? Including Aiden!"

"That's enough!" Dray's eyes went iceberg cold. "Your manners leave a lot to be desired, my dear. I don't allow children to behave this way in my house. It's time for you to leave."

The library door clicked and Nora appeared, her eyes glowing the way they always did when she'd discovered something. She took a deep breath before announcing, "They believe there's a powerful weapon that can defeat the Mara. That's what they've been hiding!"

"You don't know what you're talking about, young lady," Dray blustered.

Aiden's face dropped. "You never said anything about that. What kind of weapon is it?"

Dray pulled himself together. "I'm afraid revealing that information to you would be too dangerous. Searching for something this powerful requires care, concentration and skill and you've only been training for a few months. Leave it to the experts, boy."

"But the Mara appeared in Wendleton!" I burst out. "We need that weapon ready for next time."

"The weapon will be used by someone with a little more self-control than you, Robyn Silver," Dray snapped.

"But I trusted you . . . I showed you all my new invention ideas. . ." Aiden tailed off.

Portia flicked her hair back. "Yeah, your brilliant inventions! Why do we need them when we have the trofflegurt?"

Miss Smiting gave a faint hiss, knocking Wendy's head as she swept past so that it dropped on to Portia's foot with a crunch.

"Ow!" Portia grabbed her toe.

"In any case, with your mentor imprisoned and awaiting a hearing at Federation headquarters in Prague, I would have thought you had other things to worry about." Dray smirked.

"They've imprisoned Cryptorum!" Nora went pale. "Why would they do that?"

Dray shrugged. "No doubt he said the wrong things to the wrong people. Erasmus was never very good at diplomacy."

"Never good at lying and flattering people – that'ss what you mean!" hissed Miss Smiting. "You could help him – you have some sway with the Federation. Have you rung them and made a case for Erasmus?"

Dray fiddled with his cane. "I'm afraid I really can't get involved. I have my own reputation to think about."

Miss Smiting's eyes flashed and she looked as if she might strike him, but instead she picked up the crike's cage and swept out of the door.

I exchanged looks with Nora. "I've got what I need," she murmured, patting her pocket, which was stuffed with paper. "Let's go."

Miss Smiting had already stashed the crike inside the van before returning for the skitting. I picked up another cage while Nora held the door for us.

"What are you doing?" Dray's face darkened. "You gave those creatures to us!"

"On second thoughts – we'd rather look after them ourselves." I took the gruckle away. Nora lifted the mimicus and staggered after me.

"Wait up!" Aiden tucked his metal sphere under his arm and picked up the jooper's cage. "I'm coming with you."

Nora and me struggled to wrap the crike's tail in its fireproof blanket. Portia followed us down the steps, her eyes stormy. "You think you're so clever, Robyn Silver! I'll get you back for this."

"Whatever!" I climbed into the van beside Aiden.

The mimicus imitated Portia's stuck-up voice perfectly. "So clever, Robyn Silver! So clever, Robyn Silver!"

Portia's cheeks flamed and she shouted something else but it was lost under the revving of the van. Then Miss Smiting hit the accelerator and we rumbled out of the driveway, leaving Kesterly Manor behind.

An Enemy Needs Our Help

e were so busy watching the monsters (especially the crike, which was trying its best to shake the fire blanket off its tail) that we didn't talk much on the way back to Grimdean House. When we'd taken the creatures back to the dungeon, I fetched Pudding and we all went upstairs. Miss Smiting left us, saying she needed to telephone Prague and find out why they'd imprisoned Cryptorum.

"So the whole thing about wanting them to take those monsters was a diversion," Aiden said as we climbed the stairs. "I knew something was going on . . . your acting is terrible, Robyn."

I shrugged. "Yeah, I know." I wasn't sure what

to say. Aiden and me had been friends for ages and we'd never had an argument like this before. I didn't want to start fighting again but I couldn't pretend it hadn't happened.

"Hey!" Aiden began awkwardly. "Sorry I didn't tell you I was going to Kesterly today. Mr Dray said I could use their labs to work on my inventions ... I wanted to go to use all their equipment but I knew you'd say something rude about it."

"I probably would have," I admitted. "I just don't like those kids and I don't trust Dominic Dray."

"Rufus was nice last time we went," Nora put in. "Shame he was out this time."

"I guess." I wasn't sure about Rufus but he wasn't as bad as Portia I suppose. I flicked the lights on in Cryptorum's study. "So what's this powerful weapon, Nora? What did you find in the library?"

"This is all of it." Nora spread some crumpled sheets out on Cryptorum's desk. "I've never copied anything down so fast before! But this was the most useful thing of all." She took out a small black pocket book and flicked through the thin pages. Pictures of the most gruesome and horrible monsters were drawn inside. "It's volume five of the Monster Compendium. You know – the one that's missing from Cryptorum's library."

"I didn't know one of them was missing," I said.

"It's extremely rare!" Nora looked surprised that I didn't know this. "It was created by the great Chime illustrator Renée Kurilla, who travelled the world searching for new monsters and drawing them. Volumes one, two, three, four, six and eight are here, but no volume five."

"What happened to number seven?" Aiden asked.

"There was only one copy ever made and it was stolen by a man called Professor du Lac." Nora leafed through the little book. "Anyway, volume five has got a picture of the Mara – see!"

The pale figure with blank eyes and a grinning mouth full of shark teeth took me straight back to that moment in the playground. I swallowed and my throat thickened as if my voice would disappear all over again. The Mara might not have claws, tentacles or spines but it was still the most terrifying thing I'd ever seen.

Under the picture, it read: *There is only one Mara, monster of nightmares. Its appearance was first recorded in Ancient Egypt on the walls of several tombs. Reading its victim's thoughts, it uncovers the worst nightmare they have ever suffered before bringing it to life.*

"But all we have to do is remind ourselves that the nightmare is not really happening, right?" Aiden said. "You never really lost your voice, Robyn, and Nora never shrank."

I exchanged looks with Nora. "I guess . . . but it felt pretty real."

"The other thing I found was this information about the weapon strong enough to defeat the Mara." Nora picked up one of her sheets of scribbled notes. "It's called Helmfist's Sword, so I guess he must have been the man who created it."

"We have to find out where it is," I cried. "If we can get hold of it all our problems with the Mara will be over."

Nora ran a finger down her notes. "It didn't say where to find it and there wasn't much information. . . Maybe the Federation will know where it is. They might even be the ones who have it. If we rang them up and explained everything maybe they'd help us and let Cryptorum go."

Pudding, who was lying on the rug, jumped up and put his paws on the windowsill, growling.

I frowned. "Nothing the Federation's done so far makes me want to trust them. First they barged in here and gave us loads of orders and then they let Dominic Dray spy on us. I don't think we should tell them anything."

"Robyn's right," Aiden said, surprising me. "They don't care about us at all! They've locked Cryptorum up in their headquarters and now we have to try to beat the Mara without him which will be the most dangerous thing we've ever done."

We were all silent for a moment.

Nora turned the sheet of paper over. "I forgot about this – there's a description of Helmfist's Sword ... *made from augmented silver ... the strongest blade forged for the strongest warrior...* This was from *An Encyclopaedia of Swords, Daggers and Cudgels.* I only wish there'd been a picture."

"What's augmented?" Aiden asked.

"I think it just means the metal was improved somehow." Nora's forehead creased as she flicked through the notes.

Something pinged in my memory. "I read a book all about different sword moves ages ago and it had a list of different swords in the back." I went to Cryptorum's bookcase and searched along the line of books. Most of them had black or brown leather covers and gold-leaf writing on the spine, but I knew the one I was looking for had a red jacket. I found it on the top shelf and turned straight to the list of swords at the back. Nora and Aiden huddled round me while we scanned the pages.

Halfway down the second page, something caught my eye. "Look, it's Cryptorum's best sword. He was so mad when I borrowed it that time!" I started reading the description out loud. "*The Sword of Runes is reputed to be the finest blade ever forged. Intended for a strong warrior, this sword is said to draw dark things towards it, which poses a significant risk for a weak or less-experienced Chime. It is sometimes called Helmfist's Sword...*" I broke off, my stomach churning. "No way ... it's Helmfist's Sword!"

Nora carried on from where I'd stopped, "*And it was made for defeating the Mara. This sword has runes engraved on the blade.* I can't believe Cryptorum's sword is the one! The runes must be those swirly markings on the blade. I wonder what they mean."

Aiden shook his head. "Flipping heck, Robyn, the fact is that you used that sword on Blagdurn Heath before Christmas and this book says it's really dangerous. It draws dark things towards it – no wonder we had to fight so many kobolds and scree sags that night. Where does Cryptorum keep it? That sword could be pulling monsters towards it right now!"

Pudding started barking, his paws on the windowsill again.

"What is it, Pudding?" I rushed over, suddenly wondering if monsters were marching towards us – pulled in by the sword. Daylight was fading and a small figure was darting across the garden to the back gate. I leaned close to the glass, struggling to make out who it was.

"Children!" Miss Smiting hurried in. "What have you been doing? There is mess everywhere downstairs. Did you take things out of the cupboardss?"

"No, that wasn't us!" Aiden said.

The figure in the garden turned for a moment. It was a boy with blond hair and he was hiding something under his sleek black jacket. "It's Rufus! He's sneaked in!" I raced for the stairs, taking them two at a time. Pudding was beside me, but by the time we ran out of the back door Rufus was gone. Pudding rushed over to the back gate and pawed at the wood. I hoisted myself up and peered over the top. The street was empty.

"Rufus!" I yelled. "I know it's you!"

Miss Smiting and the others caught up with me.

"Lower your voice, Robyn," Miss Smiting told me. "What on earth iss going on?"

I climbed down. "I saw Rufus – I know it was him!" I noticed the door to the weapons shed hanging open. The hinge on the trapdoor had been broken too. "Dammit! He's taken the sword."

"What ssword?" asked Miss Smiting.

"The one that can defeat the Mara." My stomach churned. That sword had been our best chance and now Rufus had stolen it. I climbed down the ladder and rummaged through piles of bows and arrows, but there was no sign of the Sword of Runes.

"I bet that's what they were talking about when their watches beeped," Aiden said suddenly. "Rufus was sent here to break in and steal the sword. Dray knew all the time that Cryptorum's blade was the right one."

"Dray definitely knew," I sighed heavily. "He told Portia and Tristan to ask all of us about a sword. I overheard them talking about it the first time we went to Kesterly. I should have told Cryptorum and made him listen to me – maybe we could have worked out what they were up to."

Nora bit her lip. "Of course they would have known the Sword of Runes was at Grimdean because they saw you fighting with it on the heath last year. Poor Rufus!"

"Poor Rufus?! He's a thief!" I said.

"He's only stolen the sword because Dray made him," Nora replied. "And he probably doesn't know that it draws monsters towards it. We have to help him!"

"Fine!" I grabbed an extra blade and a bow and some arrows from the open shed. "We'll help him and when we've done that I'm gonna kick his butt!"

As night fell, we went to search the streets around Grimdean House. Clusters of bats swooped through the darkening sky. I had brought Pudding, pretending every time we passed someone that I was just taking him for a walk. Miss Smiting had returned to the house to try to telephone the Federation once more about releasing Cryptorum.

"Robyn!" Aiden pointed to a silver Rolls-Royce turning the corner by Grimdean House.

Dray had a car like that. I signalled to Aiden and he stepped back into the shadows. As the Rolls-Royce came closer, I spotted Dray in the driving seat and Tristan's pinched face at the window.

"I bet they've come to pick up Rufus," I said to

Aiden, once they'd gone. "You'd think they'd use something less obvious for a getaway car."

Aiden grinned. "Idiots! It's gonna make it hard though – they can cover ground a lot faster than us."

"Guys!" Nora doubled back to meet us. "I saw Rufus but he spotted me and ran down the street towards the Palavo Centre."

"The Rolls won't be able to get down there! Come on!" I called to Pudding as I started running. The Palavo Centre was a shopping precinct with no way for cars to drive in. If we were lucky, we could catch up with Rufus before Dray even worked out where he was.

We were halfway there when Dray's Rolls-Royce swung out of a side street. We dodged behind a bus shelter. The posh car circled the roundabout slowly before moving on again.

"We can't get rid of them. It's almost as if Dray knows where we are," Nora whispered.

I thought of the map I'd seen on Dray's watch and the cluster of blinking dots. "Aiden, check your Kesterly watch!"

"I checked it when he first gave it to me." Aiden undid his watch and pulled the casing off the back. "You were right – there's a tracking device.

I must've missed it the first time." He thrust the watch into a nearby bush. "That'll fool them."

As soon as the road was clear we moved on, keeping to the shadows. The shops had shut for the night when we reached Palavo Street. An empty plastic bag drifted across the pavement and a pile of spilt chips lay beside a bench. I led the way down the street, dodging behind trees and bins as much as I could, although there wasn't much cover. The plastic stares of the mannequins in the shop windows seemed to follow us.

"I'm sure he came down here." Nora gripped her torchblade tightly.

I knelt down by Pudding. "Hey, can you find Rufus?" The Chime wolf raised his nose to sniff the air, before running towards an alleyway.

There was a shape close to the alley covered with spines. A kobold! No, two kobolds.

An ear-splitting crash made the kobolds scatter. I rounded the corner at top speed and skidded to a halt nearly falling on top of a scree sag. I couldn't believe what I was seeing. Rufus had climbed on to a dustbin, surrounded by a mass of monsters including a gruckle and a jooper. He was swinging at the creatures with Cryptorum's sword, a look of panic on his face. A neon shop sign flashed above his head.

He caught sight of me. "Robyn! Help!"

I drew my torchblade and cleared a path through the kobolds with a few swings. Pudding helped me, snapping and snarling at the monsters. "Hi, thief!" I reached Rufus. "Taken anything you shouldn't have lately?"

Rufus didn't catch the sarcasm. "They all came after me! I couldn't get away."

"Behind you!" Nora yelled, as the gruckle leapt at his ankles.

The bin wobbled, unbalanced by the weight of Rufus and the jumping gruckle. Shoving the jooper out of the way with my elbow, I dashed in and grabbed Rufus as he fell. We ended up on the ground with my knee on top of his head.

"Sorry!" I pulled him to his feet. "But it serves you right for—" I stopped and stared.

The swirly markings on Cryptorum's sword glowed a fiery orange that was so bright it made my eyes hurt. I'd seen this once before. My mind flashed back to that night on Blagdurn Heath when Annie had been in danger and I'd borrowed the sword from Cryptorum without asking. The markings had glowed that night – I was sure of it.

"The Sword of Runes," I muttered to myself. "But what do the runes say?" The gruckle smacked into me, interrupting this thought. I fell, hitting my shoulder heavily against the wall. Lurching to my feet, I swung my torchblade at the gruckle but it dodged.

An arrow whizzed over my head and hit the jooper. Then another hit a kobold. Nora had climbed on to a stretch of wall and was firing silver-tipped arrows as fast as she could fit them to the bowstring. Aiden was fighting off scree sags with Pudding's help and Rufus was nursing a bruised forehead.

Swinging at the gruckle again, I landed a blow on its haunches. The creature let out a deafening howl, before springing right over my head and legging it out of the alley. The other monsters took this as a signal to run away too. A cluster of bats swooped after them. The alley emptied. Four piles of scree sag bones and an upturned dustbin were the only signs that anything had happened.

Rufus backed away from me, clutching the Sword of Runes. The fiery glow on the blade had faded. "Thanks for that! I should really be getting back now because Dray and the others will be expecting me."

I held up my torchblade, the neon light from the shop sign flashing on the metal. "You're not getting out of here with Cryptorum's sword. You know that, right?"

"You should let me take it to Kesterly Manor." The old smug expression crept back into Rufus's eyes. "You didn't even know you had something important and nor did Cryptorum. At least we'll look after this sword and use it to do what it was meant for – kill the Mara."

A gust of cold wind swept down the alley, sending empty crisp packets flying. A cluster of little black bugs crawled down the alley wall and on to Rufus's shoulder.

"Ugh!" He brushed them off hurriedly and one burst into a swirl of black smoke. Another flitted on to the sword and began crawling along the blade.

"Dream leeches!" Nora cried. "The Mara won't be far behind."

"What?" Rufus whirled round, so I stuck my foot out and tripped him. As he staggered, I pulled the sword out of his hand.

"This belongs to us," I said firmly and Pudding barked in agreement.

"Come back to Grimdean House with us and we can share what we know," Aiden said.

"No way! She's trying to kill me!" Rufus jerked his head at me.

I rolled my eyes. "I'm not trying to kill you. Don't be so overdramatic."

"You'll be OK if you come with us," Nora told him earnestly. "But we can't stay here – we have to get somewhere safe and figure all of this out."

Rufus glanced round fearfully as if the Mara might burst out of the alley wall. "OK. I'll go with you, as long as I can borrow a sword."

We Study the Sword of Runes

lent Rufus my torchblade and we left Palavo Street as fast as we could. Dray's Rolls-Royce zoomed round a corner as we got close to Grimdean House and I pulled Rufus back into the shadows.

"Why can't I show the sword to Mr Dray?" Rufus sounded like a little kid who wanted a favourite toy back.

"Because Dray doesn't really want to work together," Aiden answered. "He had me fooled too . . . but you can't trust him."

We waited till the car had disappeared before running up the Grimdean steps and dashing inside. I bolted the massive front door behind us.

"Let's have hot chocolate and cookies." Nora

led the way to the kitchen. "I'm hungry." She filled the kettle and got a packet of cookies out of the cupboard.

Rufus sat down at the kitchen table and rested his chin on his hand.

"What shall we do with him?" I hissed to Aiden and Nora. "I bet he knows more than he's saying. We have to find a way to make him tell!"

"I *am* finding a way." Nora added the chocolate powder to the mugs. "Can you pass me those little marshmallows?"

I passed her the packet. "Seriously! We need that information. There's no time to muck around."

"I'm not!" Nora whispered. "Just give me a few minutes." She set a steaming mug of hot chocolate down in front of Rufus. Little marshmallows bobbed on the top covered with a dusting of chocolate powder.

"Thanks!" Rufus nodded. "I'm really hungry."

Nora offered him a cookie and sat down opposite. "You've had an awful day. I bet you didn't even want to come here in the first place."

"I didn't!" Rufus pushed his blond hair out of his eyes. "I told Dray it should be Tristan – he's much better at sneaking around – and it took ages to find that trapdoor in the floor of your shed."

I gritted my teeth. Poor Rufus! Having to break into our shed like that.

Nora smiled and offered Rufus another cookie. "So when did Dray realize the sword was so important?"

Rufus crunched the cookie, looking thoughtful. "I think it was when those books on runes came from the Federation. He spent hours and hours going through them. That's what I was supposed to do if I couldn't fetch the sword itself – if it was chained to a wall or something. I was meant to decode the runes and let Dray know what they said." He pulled some paper from his pocket which looked like a photocopy from a book.

"May I see?" Nora spread the paper out on the table. There were rows of runes with thin spidery writing under each one.

"Dray says Chimes in the olden days discovered there were runes on Viking weapons and shields that mentioned the monsters of the Unseen World," Rufus added. "The Vikings must have thought the runes had some kind of power – so the Chimes tried using them too."

I laid the Sword of Runes on the table beside the sheet of paper. "There!" I pointed to a curved line with two prongs. "That's the first one. What does it say?"

"It means 'I am'." Nora leaned close to the paper. "The next one means 'made'."

"That one next," Aiden pointed to another. "It says 'dark'."

"Last one 'power'," I finished. "So that's: *I am made with dark power.*"

"What does that mean though?" Aiden said. "It doesn't really make sense."

"If the sword was forged with dark power that would explain why it attracts monsters and why it's so dangerous to use." Nora touched the runes etched on to the sword.

I turned to Rufus. "Dray sent you here to steal a sword that's basically a monster magnet."

Rufus smoothed back his fringe. "I don't believe you. If it was that dangerous he'd never have sent me."

"It's true!" Nora told him. "We found a description in a book which said this sword draws dark things towards it." Rufus's smug look faded. "That must be why you got cornered by so many monsters in Palavo Street. They're drawn to it somehow."

Rufus looked horrified. "I thought it was just a bad part of town. . ."

"Well at least we know the sword works." I

drank some hot chocolate. "Now we just need to get out there and use it to beat the Mara."

"We need a proper plan first. If Cryptorum was here. . ." Aiden broke off.

"But he's not here!" I pointed out.

"Robyn! The dream leech!" Aiden was staring at my arm.

I quickly brushed the bug off my sleeve, but instead of bursting into a swirl of black smoke it flitted on to the table. Suddenly, there was another crawling over Nora's mug and two more on the ceiling.

"They're not vanishing quickly like they usually do." Nora shivered. "That can only mean the Mara's power is growing."

"We could use the DED machine to track it down," Aiden said. "There are other things we could use too but they're all at Kesterly Manor."

I glared at Rufus. "Are you going to help us or are you going to run back to Dray and tell him where the sword is?"

Rufus looked serious. "I want to help. Dray lied to me too."

I glanced at Nora and she nodded.

"I'll get Miss Smiting to drive us both back there." Aiden got up. "Rufus can help me sneak in and get what I need without the others knowing."

I picked up the sword. "I'll take this. We can't leave it here while the house is empty."

"It's too dangerous to keep at your home!" Nora's eyes nearly popped. "Don't do it!"

"This is our *only way* to beat the Mara. We can't leave it here and risk someone taking it," I pointed out. "What if Dray comes back and tells Portia and Tristan to break in?"

"At least find somewhere to hide it that's not inside your house," Nora said.

"I will." Pudding whined and leaned against my leg. "I'll take Pudding too – he shouldn't be alone here either."

Miss Smiting dropped me and Nora home before driving Aiden and Rufus to Kesterly Manor. The plan was that Rufus would go in alone and fetch everything Aiden wanted without arousing suspicion. I had some doubts about whether we could really trust him but Nora seemed to – I hoped she was right.

Heading for home, I turned down the side alley with Pudding beside me. I could hear voices inside – Mum telling off my little brother Josh for pinching biscuits. Keeping low, I darted past the back door and ran to the bottom of the garden. Opening the shed, I hid the sword under an old picnic blanket at the back and piled lots of things on top of it. Then I shut the door carefully and fastened the padlock to make sure neither Josh or Annie could get in. Now I just had to find a way to sneak Pudding to my bedroom.

Telling Pudding to stay, I slipped in through the back door. Mum was by the oven stirring a stew, Dad and Ben were watching athletics on TV, Annie and Josh were fighting with plastic dinosaurs and Sammie was in her room. How was I going to get an enormous Chime wolf past them all?

"Oh, you're back, Robyn. Did you have a nice time with Nora?" Mum asked.

"Yes, great... Um... I think I dropped something outside." I slipped back out the door.

Pudding was jumping round the side alley making loud thumps by colliding with the wooden fence. "Shh, Pudding!" I whispered. "They'll come out and see you. What are you doing anyway?" I spotted a little silver mouse darting through the wolf's paws. The creature hid behind a rock and then peeked out with its spoon-shaped ears pricked up, which made Pudding get excited again.

At last, the mouse scurried through a hole in the fence and disappeared. Pudding whined, before nudging the mouse's stone, which rolled aside to reveal some buttons, a gold ring, a rusty key, Sammie's crystal earrings and a pencil.

"Oh, it's a hamling – they like collecting stuff." I gathered up the ring, the key and the earrings. "OK, this gives me an idea." Going round to the front door, I carefully pushed everything I'd found through the letter box. Then I knocked loudly on the door before running round the back with Pudding.

As I opened the kitchen door, I heard my dad's voice. "Look at this, Marie. It's my wedding ring! I thought I'd lost that at work . . . and there's other stuff here too – the missing key to that bike lock."

"Did you see who put it through the letter box?" My mum left the oven and her footsteps faded down the passageway.

I felt bad for tricking them but they wouldn't understand about the hamling as they couldn't see it and at least they had their stuff back. Calling softly to Pudding, I crept inside and padded up the stairs while they were still staring at the objects on the doormat.

I hurried the wolf into my bedroom and looked

for a hiding place. "What are we going to do, Pudding? The wardrobe's way too small and you'll never fit under my bed!" Pudding gave a soft bark and lay down on the rug. I chewed my lip. The only other choice was to bribe Annie to keep quiet. I opened the wardrobe and pulled a bag of sweets off the shelf at the top. This was where I kept things I didn't want my little sister getting her hands on. I knew Annie loved the jelly-fizz sweets as much as I did.

The floorboard outside the door creaked and I zoomed over, pulling Annie inside as soon as she opened the door. "If you can keep a secret I will give you more sweets than you can possibly imagine!" I whispered. Spotting Pudding, Annie started to gasp but I shushed her. "Pudding's staying here tonight and Mum and Dad don't know."

"Why did you bring him here?" Annie knelt down to stroke Pudding.

"Grimdean House is empty because Mr Cryptorum's gone away," I said. "I can't let Pudding stay there all alone, can I?"

"Aw!" Annie fussed Pudding's ears. "It's all right, Pudding. I won't tell anyone about you. Is he hungry?"

This was a good point. I was pretty starving so

Pudding must be too. The smell of stew drifting up the stairs wasn't helping. "I'll take some stuff for him at dinner."

"I'll go down and check no one has guessed our secret!" Annie's flushed face as she bounced out of the room made me remember how nice secrets used to be before they involved deadly monsters.

I spotted a dream leech crawling on the window sill so I pulled the window open and flicked it outside. I searched the room but there weren't any more. Pudding lifted his head and gave a faint growl. I peered at the dark outline of the shed at the bottom of the garden. Nothing was moving down there. If any monsters were drawn to the sword at least I'd have Pudding here to help me. I gave the wolf a rub and headed downstairs for some dinner.

Before I went to bed that night, I set my alarm for the next morning. I needed to get up early and meet the others at Grimdean so we could plan what to do. A picture of the Mara flashed into my mind as I closed my eyes – a black suit, shark teeth and blank white eyes. I tried to imagine myself facing the monster while holding the Sword of Runes. At least we'd found the one thing we needed to defeat it.

16

I Wake Up Cold

woke up feeling bone cold so I huddled under the duvet for a while before I remembered the alarm. Was it time yet? Bright light shone round the edges of the curtains and I jerked upright, worried I'd slept too long.

Quarter to ten! Aiden and Nora would be mad at me for keeping them waiting . . . and why wasn't Pudding here?

I got dressed and ran downstairs to the kitchen where Annie and Josh were sitting at the breakfast table.

"Look at these, Robyn," Annie said. "Josh thinks they're horrible but I think they're pretty." She held out her fingers as if she was showing me something but her hand was empty. "Don't you think they're nice?"

"There's nothing there," I told her.

"Look!" She thrust her hand right at my face. "I think it's a beetle and I'm calling him Bob."

"Off! Off! Off!" Josh flicked his finger at the table over and over.

"Don't hurt them!" Annie squealed. "I'm telling Mum."

I frowned. "Josh what are you doing?"

My little brother carried on flicking – at the table, the cereal packet and the bowls. "Getting them off the table."

"Getting what off the table?"

He looked at me as if I was mad. "The black bugs with the shiny wings."

A horrible panic squeezed my chest. He was describing the dream leeches but there weren't any here and Josh and Annie shouldn't be able to see them anyway. Was this an illusion? Was the Mara nearby playing tricks on their minds?

My heart began to race. The only way I knew to beat the Mara was by using the sword. "Stay here!" I rushed outside and ran down to the shed. My fingers were freezing and I was panicking so much that I tugged at the door over and over, forgetting I'd locked it.

Finding the key under a brick, I dived inside and lifted the picnic blanket. The sword was still there! I picked it up, feeling better as soon as I had it in my hands. I would have to face the Mara without my friends. I gripped the sword hilt tighter. I just had to remember not to fall for any of the monster's nightmare illusions, like last time when I'd believed I couldn't speak. I wasn't going to fall for that this time.

I scanned the garden. There was no sign of the Mara so I went down the alley to check the street. Annie opened the front door and I hid the sword behind my back in a hurry. "Mum's calling you," she told me.

I found Mum in the living room, sitting on the sofa and muttering to herself. "When it strikes thirteen the monster comes. . ."

"Mum, what's going on?" I stopped in the doorway, keeping the Sword of Runes behind my back.

"That's when the monster comes – did you know that? When the clock strikes thirteen." She looked at me intently. "Don't forget that the clock struck thirteen."

I sat beside her, my heart sinking. "Mum, what's wrong?"

She glanced out the window fearfully. "Your dad and Ben went after those things. . ."

A tight feeling squeezed my insides. "They went after what things?"

Mum's face flickered and suddenly she turned into my teacher, Mrs Perez, with her neat dark hair and glasses. "Robyn Silver! Do concentrate on your embroidery. You have to make sure each stitch is the same size and the edging must all line up smartly."

I gaped. The Sword of Runes had disappeared and on my lap lay a piece of cloth stitched with pink cotton. The cloth was bunched up where some of the stitches had been pulled too tight. I lifted the needle in my hand. "I don't even know what to do. . ."

"Don't you want to make your parents proud of you, Robyn?" Mrs Perez said sternly. "Finish every single stitch, please, and then we can begin your cheerleading lesson."

"What?!" I looked down again and suddenly I was wearing a disgusting-looking short red skirt and holding two shiny pom-poms. What was going on? I didn't have time for this! Jumping up, I dropped the pom-poms and ran outside.

I scanned the street, the front gardens and the

parked cars. There was no sign of Dad, Ben or the Mara but the Sword of Runes was back in my hand. It was so cold today and the silence made my skin prickle. I was starting to wonder where everyone was when I heard a faint noise in the distance growing steadily louder. Dad and Ben appeared, sprinting up the middle of the road between the parked cars. I hadn't seen my dad run like that since Annie was a baby and Josh had taken the brake off her pram and let her roll away down the hill.

"Get inside, Robyn!" My dad gasped. "There are monsters!"

So he was under the Mara's illusion too. I had to get them out of the way so I could face the Mara alone. "There's nothing there, Dad," I called. "Don't worry I can take care of things."

His face was red from running and shouting. "No, Robyn – get in! Tell Josh and Annie to stay away from the windows."

"Watch it – a skeleton!" Ben yelled, swerving to the right. He flew sideways as if something had barrelled into him, but then he managed to regain his balance and keep running.

My dad had fallen behind and I hurried into the road to meet him. My chest tightened. This was all my fault – I'd brought the sword here and the Mara must have followed it. If I went far away maybe I could take the nightmare monster with me.

"Dad – the bull!" Ben shouted.

My dad turned, his eyes fixing on the monster illusion I couldn't see. Putting on a burst of speed, he grabbed me and pulled me round the side of a car.

"Dad, it's OK—"

BANG! Something hit the car so hard the whole thing shuddered. My heart missed a beat. Scrambling up, I dashed round the side to find two huge gouge marks. Whatever made them was mean and heavy and had horns.

A grodder? It couldn't be. . . But illusions didn't make gouge marks in cars. Whatever did this was real.

"Does it look like a giant bull with burning red eyes?" I asked.

"Of course it does – it's right there!" Ben seized my arm, pulling me through the garden gate.

Dad closed the gate behind us. A second later it was smashed off its hinges and trampled to the ground.

"And are there bony things – a bit like skeletons but with white lips and black eyes?" I asked.

Ben thrust the front door open and shoved me inside. "Yes! Don't look at them, OK?"

"And are there small spiny things with sharp teeth that smell disgusting?"

"Robyn – there are weird creatures everywhere!" Dad slammed the door. "Now for goodness' sake go and look after Josh and Annie, and don't let them look outside – they'll be terrified. And put that silly toy sword away."

I clung on to the wall as the world rocked. Everything was wrong. I was supposed to be the only one that saw the monsters. I knew how to fight – to keep people safe. Now I was the only one who couldn't see the grodders, the kobolds and the scree sags. How could I protect my family when I was blind to danger?

Running upstairs, I went to my bedroom window. The street was still empty but now I knew that was a lie. There were monsters down there that were invisible to me. I gripped the windowsill, my hands like ice. I couldn't protect Annie or Josh – I couldn't protect anyone. This was my worst nightmare.

Wait a second. . .

This was MY worst nightmare – the embroidery, the cheerleading AND not being able to see the monsters.

What if *I* was the one under an illusion? I pinched myself but my skin was so frozen I could hardly feel it. I shut my eyes and opened them again.

Nothing had changed.

If this wasn't real how was I going to snap myself out of it?

I went to the bathroom and splashed water on my face but that just made me colder. As I stood in front of the mirror, I began to shake from side to side.

"Robyn!" It was Sammie's voice and it sounded as if she was calling me from a distance. "Robyn, wake up."

The shaking got stronger.

I sat up in the dark. I was still in bed and a black shape was looming over me. "What the heck. . . ?"

"Shh!" Sammie said fiercely. "Come downstairs right now and don't wake Annie."

A shaky relief washed over me. I'd had a nightmare. None of it had been real. I could still see monsters and I didn't have to do any embroidery or wave those stupid cheerleading pom-poms. I pulled on my dressing gown. I should have realized that none of it was true – I'd felt so cold and unreal in the dream. I glanced down and found four dream leeches crawling over my dressing-gown sleeve.

"Hurry up!" Sammie hissed from the doorway. Luckily in the gloom she hadn't noticed Pudding curled up by the radiator with his head between his paws.

I followed her downstairs and she closed the kitchen door behind us. "What do you think you're doing with this?" She pointed to the Sword of Runes, which was lying on the table, its blade gleaming in the kitchen light.

"Where did you get that?" I reached for it but she blocked my way.

"I saw you from the window when you went into the shed yesterday. So when I woke up and heard noises in the garden I thought it was you, but when I went out to check there was no one there. Then I found this hidden under a blanket." She glared at me. "You know this is a real sword and it's sharp, right? So where did you steal it from?"

"I didn't steal it." I reached for it again but Sammie pushed me back. "I'm just looking after it while Mr Cryptorum's away and he'll be cross if you touch it, so give it back."

She raised her eyebrows. "So you pinched it from Cryptorum. Wow, when he finds out he's really not going to want you in his Bat Club any more."

A dream leech landed on the kitchen table

and crawled along the blade. I glanced round nervously. "It shouldn't be brought into the house. You don't understand. . ."

"That it's dangerous?" She folded her arms. "I think I understand a lot better than you."

Just behind her shoulder, a patch of wall began to darken. "Sammie, the thing is—"

"Mr Cryptorum's spent all this time and attention on you – which is what you're always trying to get from Mum and Dad," she carried on. "And you're going to be grounded for so long when they find out what you've done."

The patch of shadow behind her darkened into the shape of a man in a black suit. His skin was paper-white, his eyes were blank and rows of shark-like teeth glinted as he smiled. Dizziness washed over me just like it had the first time I'd seen the Mara. I tried to pull my sister away but she pushed me back, her face pinched with fury. "You're NOT having this sword back. You're just a stupid little girl playing adventures."

"I'm not!" I gasped. "I need that sword! I can't explain why." I broke off as the Mara moved closer to her. "Sammie, come over here!"

"She can't see me." The Mara's mouth didn't move but I could hear his voice inside my head, sharp as a nail dragged over a windowpane. "And your sword won't help you, Robyn Silver. No Chime relic can hurt me now."

I shivered. I hadn't expected the monster to know my name.

"What's that?" Sammie cried.

For a second I thought she'd heard the Mara's voice, but she rushed to the window. In the darkness outside, something taller than a tree lumbered up the road. It passed under a street lamp and a thick black body supported by a clutch of hairy legs came into view – a giant spider, like something from a horror movie, except this one had wings.

"It's a nightmare spider!" I said. "Like the one Nora's mum dreamed about. It's just an illusion – you've made it up."

"What are you talking about?" snapped Sammie. "There are no such things as nightmare spiders." She ran down the hallway and opened the front door to look.

"Humans!" The Mara smiled. "With your books and your movies, you have more monsters in your imaginations than ever before and you have made me strong. I have spent weeks collecting the dream leeches that each of you produced in your sleep. I have gathered them together and harnessed their power. These are not illusions any more. I have grown strong enough to make your nightmares real."

He clicked his fingers and the street lamp glowed fiercely. Behind the giant spider, a horrible-looking ogre with long brown tusks lumbered down the road. A group of people with rat heads and tails crept after them. Wendleton's nightmares were coming alive.

I snatched up the Sword of Runes. Raising it over my head, I swung at the Nightmare Man as hard as I could. The blade sliced through him as if he was made of air and he stood there grinning, completely unhurt.

"No Chime relic can stop me now because your nightmares are real," he said. "This is my time and it will last for ever."

Another wave of dizziness washed over me and I dropped the sword on the table. When I looked up, Sammie had run back inside and the Mara was gone.

Nightmares Chase Me Across Town

I couldn't remember how many times I'd wished Sammie would stop moaning at me. Considering how often we'd argued it had to be millions of times but now she wasn't speaking at all and that was worse. Gripping the curtain tightly, she pressed her eye to the tiny gap between the wall and the drapes and watched the procession of nightmares outside.

"Don't look any more," I told her. "It'll be better if you don't see them."

A thudding sound came from the street and she breathed in sharply. "It won't be better," she whispered. "I'll still know they're out there. These things shouldn't be loose... They must have broken out of a science lab or a secret government experiment. There must be something on the news!"

A padding noise came from the stairs and Sammie shrieked as Pudding came in. "You kept that dog here?" Pudding sniffed at the window and growled softly. "Actually, I really don't care!" She grabbed the remote control and started flicking through the TV channels, looking for news of a mass escape from a science lab.

"Robyn, help!" Annie squeaked from upstairs.

Taking the stairs two at a time, I burst into our room to find Annie curled up on the bed while her toys raced round the bedroom floor, raining blows on each other.

"They won't stop fighting!" Tears welled in my little sister's eyes. "Make them stop, Robyn."

I swallowed. Of course – this must be her nightmare that was now real. "OK, don't worry." I tried to separate the crazy come-to-life toys, but the pink bear kept jumping on the elephant's head and the fluffy unicorn ran away with one of the doll's arms. "Annie, let's go downstairs." I lifted her off the bed and she buried her head in my shoulder. Taking her into the living room, I found Ben sitting on the sofa and Josh hiding in the corner with green skin and two alien antennae sprouting from his head. Sammie was still flicking through the TV channels and Pudding was at the window, growling.

"I can't move!" Ben croaked. "I'm just stuck here. I've tried to move but I can't. It feels like I'll never move again."

I set Annie down and tried pulling Ben up but it was no use. I heard a cry from the kitchen and let his hands drop. "I'm sorry!" I dashed next door to find my mum trapped under dozens of washing baskets all full of clothes. I tried to pull them away from her but they weighed a tonne.

I looked round, despairing. These were their nightmares. Mum was trapped under laundry, Josh was an alien, Ben couldn't move and Annie's toys were fighting each other. "Where's Dad?" I asked.

"Outside. He can't get the car started," Mum said weakly from underneath the pile of baskets. "I don't understand! This is like a horrible dream."

"Don't worry, I'm going to fix it." I crouched down and held her hand. A broken revving noise came from the street – it had to be Dad working on the car. Trust him to have the most boring nightmare of all. But what about Sammie – what was her most terrifying dream? I ran back to the living room where Sammie was staring at the TV with a dazed expression.

"What nightmares have you had lately?" I demanded.

"What do you mean?" She frowned.

"Nightmares! What's made you scared in your sleep?"

A look of horror took over her face. "Is that what's going on? How is it possible?"

"Never mind that. What's your worst nightmare? Tell me quickly."

A white shape passed the window. A few seconds later there was a thumping on the front door.

Sammie shut her eyes. "It can't be – it can't be!"

The door flung open and a giant white rabbit stooped to squeeze through the entrance. It walked on two legs like a great fluffy toy come to life. Annie squealed and ran to the kitchen while Josh shrank further into the corner. The bunny had huge wiry whiskers, each one as thick as a pencil, deep black eyes and an empty basket over its arm. It glared at Sammie, roaring, "Chocolate!"

I looked at Sammie. "This is your worst nightmare? Seriously?"

"It's Ben's fault! I was really excited about Easter one year when I was little." Sammie dodged behind the sofa. "Then he told me that the Easter Bunny collected chocolate instead of giving it out and if I was awake when he came in the night he'd carry me away."

"I was only kidding." Ben tried to pull himself up. "It's not real though, is it?"

"It's real," I told them.

"Chocolate!" growled the rabbit, advancing on Sammie.

"Run, Sammie!" I launched myself at the rabbit, bouncing off its massive white stomach and falling to the floor.

Pudding leapt forward but the Easter Bunny swept him aside with one swipe of its giant paw. The rabbit stepped over me, lifted Sammie into the air and swung her over one shoulder. Then, in a few strides, the creature was out of the door.

"Robyn, help!" Sammie cried, as she and the rabbit disappeared into the dark.

"I'm coming!" I dodged round Ben, who was trying to heave himself up so much that he nearly pulled the whole sofa over. Grabbing the Sword of Runes from the kitchen, I ran out into the night.

Lights were switching on in houses up and

down the street and scared faces peered from bedroom windows. I ducked behind our hedge and scanned the road. The only nightmare I could see was a crocodile in a bonnet pushing a supermarket trolley with squeaky wheels. It stopped and stared as my dad got out of his car and marched back into the house. I held my breath, ready to run to his defence, but my dad (who was muttering about dodgy motors) went inside without noticing anything. There was a moment of silence before the squeaking of the trolley started up again.

When the squeaking grew fainter, I ran out into the middle of the road. Sammie and the white rabbit had disappeared and when I reached the crossroads I still couldn't see them. I couldn't stop picturing the look of fear on my sister's face. It was true me and Sammie didn't always get on but this world of monsters was my world and it was up to me to save her.

The best way to get her back was to go to Grimdean and get Aiden and Nora's help. Fur brushed against my hand and I found Pudding at my side. "Good boy!" I whispered. "Let's go."

Creeping down the road, we stopped to hide whenever a swarm of dream leeches passed overhead. I was afraid they might be able to tell the Mara where I was somehow or that each of them could turn into a full-sized nightmare at any moment.

When we reached my old school, I nearly dropped the Sword of Runes. The whole place, which had been a building site for months, was overrun by garden gnomes. They were swinging from the scaffolding, dancing in the wheelbarrows and practising karate in the playground. I watched until some of them spotted me and gave chase. One leapt out of a tree at me and I parried with the sword, sending it smashing to the pavement. A wild, whooping cry went up from the rest of the gnomes. They hurtled at us, their round faces red with fury, so me and Pudding ran for it.

The grey shape of Grimdean House had never looked so welcoming. I sped up, dodging a block of bad-smelling cheese the size of a horse which was sliding across the pavement. As I reached the steps, a nurse holding a needle grabbed my arm. Pudding snapped at her but she held on tight, saying, "Stand still! This won't take a moment."

Aiden opened the Grimdean front door. "Robyn, quick!"

Pudding raced inside and I tore myself free and ran after him.

Aiden slammed the door shut. He, Nora and Rufus all had frostblades and Nora had a bow slung over her shoulder. A mass of gadgets, wires and tools lay on the floor. Wendy, the Kesterly training robot, sat propped against a wall with her head slumped to her chest.

"The Mara was in my house!" I panted. "It told me that it's so strong it can bring nightmares to life. These aren't illusions any more. They're real."

"I figured that out when a giant crab did this to me." Aiden lifted a bandage to show me a cut on his arm.

"What did the Mara do, Robyn?" Nora twisted her plait. "Did you try the sword?"

"It's useless!" I glanced at the runes on the blade, which hadn't glowed since we'd saved Rufus in the alley. "I struck the Mara and it went straight through him. Then he told me *'No Chime relic can stop me now,'* and *'This is my time and it will last for ever'.*"

"He's taken over the town," Rufus said. "There were nightmares everywhere as we drove back from Kesterly Manor."

"*'This is my time'*," Nora repeated. "That's strange! If he was boasting why didn't he say *'This is my town now'*, or something like that?"

"I am ssorry, my dears." Miss Smiting hurried down the stairs. "I have been trying to reach you but there was a two-headed wraith-gator in the corridor." She shivered.

I realized I'd never seen Miss Smiting look scared before. "We need Cryptorum. Nothing's been right since he left for Prague."

"Yeah, that was when the clock stopped working too," Aiden put in. "It's weird if you think about it – almost as if the monsters knew he was gone."

"Your Mortal Clock stopped working?" Rufus's eyebrows rose. "Isn't that a *really* bad sign?"

"Worse than living nightmares roaming the streets, you mean?" I rolled my eyes.

"No, he's right!" Nora said. "The Mortal Clock contains Chime power and the Mara's been growing stronger ever since it broke. He may have been the one to break it."

"You mean this might not have happened if the clock was still working?" I tried to get my head round that idea. "I dreamt about this! Actually my mum said it to me in the dream. She said, 'When the clock strikes thirteen the monster comes,' and that's exactly what happened. The clock struck thirteen before it stopped working!"

"So if we can fix the clock it'll restore the Chime

power in this town and we may have a chance of beating the nightmares," Nora said.

We all looked at Aiden.

"I can't fix it – I've tried!" he said. "Every time I thought I'd got it working the mechanism broke down again."

"That iss not the only obstacle," Miss Smiting told us. "I have been past the tower door and there are huge holes in the passageway."

Nora shuddered. "Falling down a hole is my biggest nightmare. Ever since my parents took me caving in the Black Mountains and I got stuck down a hole in the dark."

"That must be why they've appeared. You and Rufus stay here and stop any nightmares getting through that door," I told them. "Me and Aiden will go up the tower."

"I really don't think I'll be able to do it," Aiden said.

"I believe in you," I told him. "If anyone can make the Mortal Clock work again, it's you."

We Go Inside the Mortal Clock

Aiden bent down just as a low rumbling started below our feet. "It's the hell wurm!" He hurriedly scooped up his tools.

"How do you know?" I asked.

"Because that's *my* worst nightmare." He started running. "Everyone get back! The wurm's coming through."

A colossal slimy wurm erupted from beneath us, showering the place with earth and broken floor tiles. A tonne of mud hit Miss Smiting and Rufus seized her hand to stop her falling into the wurm hole. Aiden dived for the safety of the stairs and I ran after him before realizing I'd lost Pudding. The Chime wolf stood his ground, barking fiercely at the monster.

"Pudding!" I turned back but more cracks opened in the floor cutting the hallway in two and leaving Rufus, Nora and Miss Smiting trapped by the front door with Pudding. The wurm swung its head to and fro as if it was tasting the air.

Aiden ducked behind the bannisters, his hands gripping the rails. "Wendy – activate!"

Wendy jerked upright and began marching across the only clear patch of floor. "Warning! Wurm tremors detected. Warning!"

"We know there's a wurm!" Aiden shouted. "Do your job and fight it."

Wendy tripped over a clump of earth and fell to her knees. "Warning! Wurm tremors detected!"

"It's all right," Nora called. "You guys go! Rufus and I can keep it busy." She pulled her bow off her shoulder and let off a volley of arrows. The wurm swung in her direction and she aimed more arrows into its jaws.

Aiden and me raced up flight after flight of stairs till we reached the passage that led to the tower. Holes were opening and closing in the floor and when I looked down all I could see was blackness like looking into outer space. Aiden pulled me back as a new hole opened at my feet and a hall table toppled into the nothingness.

"We have to do this quickly." I jumped to the next bit of solid floor and kept going. I didn't even want to think about what would happen if a hole opened when I was halfway across. The last hole was double the size of the others but once we'd jumped it the rest of the floor was solid. Reaching the door to the tower, we ran up the spiral stairs to the clock room at the top.

I'd never been inside the clock tower before and my mouth dropped open when I saw it. Clockwork filled the whole room – spreading over the walls and most of the floor. Huge cogs fitted into one another linking one part of the machinery to the next. A massive golden wheel, taller than me, stood at the centre of the workings.

Aiden nodded to it. "That pulls the bell rope to make the clock chime." I followed his gaze to the enormous gold bell that hung below the rafters. "But when I came up here before I couldn't figure out why it wasn't working. Nothing looks broken – the weight's in place and all the clockwork should be running. . ."

"How is a Mortal Clock different from normal clocks?" I interrupted. "I mean – it woke our powers at midnight so there must be something special about it, right?"

"I asked Miss Smiting about that the first time I tried to mend it. She didn't know and Nora said she hadn't read anything about it."

"Maybe it's a Chime Federation secret." I edged between the cog wheels, looking for anything strange. I'd never seen the machinery of a clock before so I wasn't sure what I was looking for. "Chime power works at midnight, doesn't it? Maybe if we move the clock hands to point to twelve that will make the clock chime and break the Mara's power."

Aiden looked at me as though I was mad. "OK so all we have to do is get hold of a fire engine with a crane or learn how to fly!"

I gazed at the back of the huge golden clock face. An iron frame held the clock hands and numbers in place. Behind the frame, the face of the clock was made from yellow glass. Moonlight shone through, casting a pool of gold light on to the wooden floor. "Oh! Can't you move the hands from here then?"

"No, you can't reach them."

I could see he was right. Opening a narrow window, I peered outside. The clock face was just round the corner of the tower. A thin ledge ran along the tower wall and I was pretty sure I could use it to climb along. Leaving the Sword of Runes on the floor, I hoisted myself on to the windowsill before swinging my feet out and feeling for the ledge with my toes.

"Robyn, don't be stupid!" Aiden cried. "It's not worth it. We don't even know if moving the clock hands will work!"

I tightrope-walked along the ledge to the corner. "Don't worry – I'm fine."

I wasn't fine. The ground looked about a million miles away. From here I could see right across Wendleton and there was weird stuff going on all over the place – a walking tree was trashing the benches in the Town Square and by the corner shop a man was fighting a huge carnivorous jelly using a bottle of washing-up liquid. But there no sign of the giant white rabbit that had taken Sammie. I wobbled and grabbed at the tower wall, hooking my fingertips into gaps in the brickwork. I mustn't look down.

Edging my way round the corner, I reached the clock face. Here the iron frame that supported the hands and numbers made it easy to climb. Pulling myself up, I took the smallest clock hand, which was pointing to five, and pushed it round the clock till it pointed to twelve.

Then I took hold of the longer hand. It was stiff so I pushed hard and the hand moved a tiny bit. Then it dropped like a stone, bashing into my legs and knocking me off the iron frame. I shrieked and managed to grab hold of the clock. My heart jumped like a kobold on a trampoline as I dangled there, clinging desperately to the long hand.

"Swing your legs up!" Aiden shouted from the window.

"I'll fall!" I yelled back.

"There's a rail on your right."

I caught a glimpse of the hell wurm below me bursting out of Grimdean's front door. My head swam and my fingers slipped a little on the metal hand.

"Robyn, go for the rail," Aiden called again.

I got my feet on to the rail and did a desperate scramble to regain my balance. With a deep breath, I took hold of the clock hand again.

"You're not still trying to do that, are you?" Aiden said. "For goodness' sake, Robyn!"

"One more try!" I pushed up the hand. Quarter to midnight ... ten to midnight ... five minutes to midnight. . . With a massive effort, I got the hand to midnight. There was a loud clunk from the machinery inside the tower and Aiden shouted something. Then there was a whirring and the clock chimed once and then stopped.

"Ugh! That was no use." I pushed the clock hand a bit more but it didn't chime again. I was sure we needed it to chime twelve times – everything about Mortal Clocks was to do with chiming midnight. I edged back along the ledge and climbed in the window. "You were right. That was just a waste of time."

"No it wasn't!" Aiden was crouched down by the golden wheel with his screwdriver. "When the clock chimed I saw this little door – it sort of lit up somehow. I just can't get it open. . ."

I leaned in to look and just behind the gold wheel there was a square hatch in the floor with bluish-white light seeping around the edges. Aiden dug his screwdriver into the keyhole, his face frozen in concentration. After a minute of twisting and turning, something clicked and Aiden pulled the hatch open triumphantly. "You can do just about anything with a screwdriver!"

A narrow passage sloped gently downwards, lit by the strange bluish light.

"It's just another passage like the ones in the walls. Maybe the light's coming from the room it leads to."

"It lit up at the exact moment the clock chimed." Aiden lowered himself inside.

I followed him in reluctantly. I could see how narrow the hole was and I hated the thought of being stuck in a tight space. We crawled, as the passage was too small to stand up, and I felt as if the sides were pressing in on me. If we came to a dead end there'd be no way to turn round. "Can you see anything?"

"Just more passageway." Aiden's voice was muffled. "But the light's definitely getting brighter."

Just then the floor creaked and gave way and we fell. I flung out my arms and smashed into the hard floor below like a starfish thrown against a rock. Aiden groaned.

"Jeez!" I dragged myself up. Everything hurt from my chin to my ankles. "I'm going to have serious words with Cryptorum when he gets back about the dangerous trapdoors in this place. Where are we now?" I caught sight of a glowing blue object in the centre of the room just before the bluish-white light that had guided us down the passage faded and went out, leaving us in darkness.

Aiden switched on the torch part of his torchblade and shone it around. The small room was filled with clockwork. Cogs and levers ran along the walls and across most of the ceiling. A glass pedestal stood in the centre of the room and an oddly shaped blue thing lay on top of it. Moonlight shone through a grate in the ceiling, giving a glimpse of the yellow clock face above. I peered at the blue thing on the pedestal. It looked like a punctured football – all weird and misshapen. "Is that what the light was coming from?"

Aiden wasn't listening. "This is so cool! We're actually inside the workings of the clock." He padded round the room, gazing in fascination. "There's a lot of spider's webs." He brushed his hand over his hair, then shone his torch round again. This time dozens of little gold strands were caught in the beam, most of them hanging from the ceiling above the glass pedestal. Some stretched right down to touch the strange blue object on top of the column.

"These aren't webs." I touched one and my fingers tingled. "Do you think they have something to do with that blue thing? I'm sure it was where the light was coming from." I climbed on the base of the pedestal to get a better look and when I touched the blue shape it felt horribly squidgy and warm.

"Robyn? Aiden?" Nora's voice came from somewhere above us in the tower.

"We're down here – use the hatch in the floor!" I yelled back.

There was a muffled thumping and first Nora and then Rufus lowered themselves down the hole that we'd fallen through. Their clothes were covered with mud. I could hear Pudding barking in the room above.

"We beat the wurm," Nora said breathlessly. "But floating jellyfish have filled the entrance hall and we had to run. They're really mean and they sting!" She showed us her arm, which was covered with red bumps. "We left Miss Smiting downstairs. She said she wouldn't be able to jump the holes in the floor."

Rufus stared at the column with the mottled blue thing. "What IS that?"

"Something pretty important." Aiden told them how it had lit up after the clock chimed. "But I don't see how it fits in with the rest of the clockwork. I've never seen a clock with something like that in the middle."

"Hold on a minute!" My stomach tumbled over. "Remember that inspector from the Federation who came to read us all those rules? Remember how he asked Cryptorum if the heart of the clock was still functioning?" I stared at the wrinkled blue thing. "Maybe this is it – this is the heart of the clock – and it's stopped working!" The more I thought about it the more I was sure I was right. It was completely weird, having a heart in the middle of a clock, but I was used to the Chime world being strange by now.

Nora's forehead wrinkled. "Are you saying that the heart of the clock is a real heart?"

"Yes! I've touched it and it's warm. It has to be a monster's heart." I took Aiden's torch and held it close to the blue heart. Now I could see the layers of flesh all knobbly and strange.

"That's horrible!" Nora shivered. "Which monster do you think it comes from?"

"I can find out for you." Rufus pushed his sleeve back and started typing things into his watch. "There's a whole monster database in here." We crowded round, watching Rufus type *blue heart* into the watch. "'*The only creature with a blue heart is the skyling that lives in the Himalayan mountains. It has the strongest heart of any creature of the Unseen World and it has been hunted heavily because. . .*' Bother! The rest is encrypted."

"Let me try!" Nora unclipped the watch and

typed on to the touchscreen. An image appeared and she enlarged it. "I couldn't get the rest of the description but I got this!" She showed us a picture of a glowing blue heart connected to clockwork by dozens of gold threads.

"The heart has to be linked up by those threads." I climbed on to the glass pedestal and grasped a thread that was dangling just above me. My fingers tingled again as I pulled the strand towards the monster's heart and pushed it in firmly.

Aiden and Rufus helped me with the gold threads while Nora climbed back through the ceiling hatch into the room above.

"It's getting out of control in town," Nora called down to us. "There are giants breaking the shop windows in the High Street. And ... oh my gosh ... Mrs Lovell is being chased by lions."

Grabbing one gold thread after another, I pushed them into the monster's heart as fast as I could. I tried not to picture Annie terrified by her toys, Ben stuck to the sofa or my mum trapped under the huge washing basket pile. I had no idea where the white rabbit might have taken Sammie. I pushed the last thread in and jumped down off the glass pedestal. Slowly, the blue heart started to gleam and white light poured out of it.

I waited for the clock chimes but nothing came. "Why isn't it chiming midnight?" I called to Nora. There was a series of thumps and Pudding barked wildly. "Aiden, give me a boost."

Aiden boosted me and I scrambled through the hatch and along the tiny passageway. Nora was on the floor fighting off a giant spider. Pudding was struggling under the biggest, stickiest web I'd ever seen. I grabbed a bow and shot an arrow into the spider's back, sending it shrieking down the stairs.

"Poor Pudding!" I pulled the web off his nose.

"Thanks!" Nora shuddered. "The long hand on the clock has slipped to three. That's why it isn't chiming."

Cursing, I climbed back on to the ledge and tightrope-walked round to the clock face again. Shrieks and yells drifted up from the street. Nightmare lions were chasing Mrs Lovell towards Grimdean House. If I didn't hurry our head teacher would be a lion's breakfast. I pushed the clock hand till it pointed to midnight.

There was a great clunking and whirring inside. I held my breath. *Bong! Bong!* The clock went on chiming until it struck twelve.

A wild gust of wind swirled around the clock

tower and I clung on desperately. Then the wind faded away, leaving an eerie silence. Mrs Lovell, who'd been screeching a moment before, looked round in confusion. The lions snapped at her but she gazed round unseeing, before turning away.

By the corner shop, the man fighting the jelly stopped hitting it with the washing-up liquid and walked off too. All across Wendleton, people ignored the nightmares and wandered back to their houses. It was clear they couldn't see the nightmares any more.

"We did it!" Nora shouted. "We broke the Mara's power!"

I edged back to the window and swung myself inside. Something was bothering me. If the Mara's power was gone why were the nightmares still here?

The lions padded along the road towards Grimdean House. The giants stepped over the row of houses, reaching Demus Street with one huge stride. The walking tree, the big carnivorous jelly, the crocodile in a bonnet and the ferocious garden gnomes each came walking, sliding, wheeling a squeaky trolley or skipping down the path with squeals of bloodthirsty delight.

"Er, guys?" I ducked my head inside. "People

aren't being chased by the nightmares any more but—"

"YAY!" Nora beamed and grabbed Aiden's hand as he emerged from the passage covered in dust. "I was worried it would be harder than that. Those holes in the upstairs corridor were *horrible*."

I peered out of the window. A patch of air by the Grimdean front door shimmered and the Mara appeared. Slowly, he lifted his head to stare at me with those horrible blank eyes. I dodged back, my heart pounding. "The nightmares. . . People can't see them but. . ."

"You never told us what your nightmare was, Rufus," Nora interrupted. "Go on! Was it something embarrassing?"

Rufus went red. "It probably sounds really stupid but I used to be afraid of garden gnomes. I think it was their shiny red cheeks and weird hats."

Aiden burst out laughing.

"Don't forget their little white beards!" Nora grinned.

"GUYS!" I yelled. "I hate to break up the party but the nightmares haven't gone – it's just that we're the only ones who can see them."

"You're kidding!" Aiden dashed to the window and the others crowded behind him.

"There are gnomes down there too." Rufus looked sick. "They're coming for us!"

I picked up the Sword of Runes. "The only thing we can do is go and face them."

19

I Battle the Easter Bunny

raced down from the tower, dodging the jellyfish floating up the stairs. A pounding noise came from below as if one of the giants was breaking in and I reached the hallway just as the front door began to buckle. The dead wurm lay coiled across the cracked floor, its tail resting against a ripped painting. I had a sudden image of how mad Cryptorum would be when he saw the destruction. "Where's Miss Smiting?" I muttered to Aiden but he shook his head.

Three more bangs and the door finally crumpled, knocked in by a massive giant's fist. The Mara strolled inside, his blank white eyes taking in the state of the hall. Dream leeches crawled over his hair and down his sleeves. "You've had a busy night, Chime children, but now you must give me that Sword of Runes."

"No way!" Rufus shouted before I could speak. "You'll *never* get the sword. We'll never let you have it!"

"Is that so?" The Mara smiled, revealing his shark teeth. "You may have broken my spell over people's minds but you are still outnumbered. So perhaps you'd like to reconsider?" He waved to the gnomes and they jumped over the rubble wielding table forks.

Rufus shrank back. I scanned the rest of the nightmares crowding up the front steps. The Mara was dead right about us being outnumbered.

Aiden whispered in my ear. "If he wants the sword it must still have its power."

I nodded slightly. The sword had run right through the Mara without hurting him before but now his spell over the human world was broken it might work the way we'd hoped. I just needed to get close enough. I stepped forward, holding out the blade. "All right! I'll give you the sword."

"Lay it on the ground." The Mara's smile vanished. "And do not seek to trick me again, Robyn Silver. I know my way round people's minds and yours is simpler than most – filled with thoughts of pizza and annoyance with your brothers and sisters." He turned his head. "Good. Bring her here."

The giants, the crocodile and all the other nightmares stood aside and the enormous white rabbit marched through carrying Sammie on his back. He dumped my sister down as if she was a sack of earth. "Chocolate!" he growled and pointed to his still-empty basket.

"Sammie, are you OK?" I tried to get to her but the Mara moved in between us.

Sammie pushed her hair out of her face. "Robyn! How did I get here? Did you play one of your stupid tricks on me?"

"No, I promise I didn't!" I swallowed. "Go home. I'll be back soon . . . I'm just finishing something."

Sammie got up but the Mara seized her wrist and stopped her from leaving. My hand tightened on my sword hilt. The Mara smiled. "You can't strike me without your sister getting hurt. If you want to save her, give me the sword."

Sammie shivered. "It's so cold. What time is it? Did the clock strike midnight?"

"Let her go," I told the Mara. "She's got nothing to do with this."

"That's not quite true, is it?" The Mara crooked his finger and the nightmares edged closer. "*She's* here because *you're* here. She's in danger because you're a Chime."

I swallowed. It was true. Sammie was here because of me. I had taken the Sword of Runes to our house and the Mara had followed me because of it.

"Give me the sword!" The Mara fixed me with his blank glare. "Your sister may not be able to see me or these nightmares any more, but she can still see everything you do. If you fight us she will know what you are . . . and I will make sure every nightmare she has from this day onwards is about you."

"Who are you talking to?" Sammie started to look annoyed with me. "Tell me what's going on."

I bit my lip. I'd spent so much time protecting my family from the Unseen World and keeping my Chime life secret. If Sammie knew what I was there was no way she'd stay quiet about it. She'd never kept a single secret of mine.

"She'll tell everyone." Rufus echoed my thoughts. "You should give him the sword. We've already broken the nightmare's spell."

"Don't do it," Aiden whispered. "The sword

could be our only chance." He leaned down and pulled a metal shape from the rubble. Wendy's face was dented and her bodywork covered in mud but there was still a crackle of electricity in her eyes.

"But if my secret gets out yours will too!" I looked from Nora to Aiden. "What about your mum? What about Bat Club?" I could see the answer in their eyes – this was a trick and if Sammie ended up knowing everything then that was the way it had to be. I turned back to the Mara. "The only way you'll get this sword is by fighting me." As I finished speaking, the runes on the sword glowed like fire. It took my breath away for a second.

The Mara released Sammie's wrist. "GET THEM!"

The nightmares attacked. First to reach us were the gnomes, who clambered the broken walls and swung from brick to brick, shaking their table forks. Next came the giants, picking up handfuls of floor tiles and smashing them against the ceiling. Then came the huge carnivorous jelly, the croc in the bonnet and dozens more nightmares from the spooky to the blow-your-mind weird. Sammie looked at me and the other Chimes, a puzzled line forming in the middle of her forehead. "Put that stupid sword down, Robyn. You look like you're trying to star in a really bad action movie."

"I wish I was!" I muttered.

"Wendy – activate!" Aiden shouted, and Wendy straightened, drawing a pair of sabres from her back.

Rufus flicked on his ultrasonic blade and dashed into battle, disappearing under a swarming mass of gnomes. Aiden wrestled the crocodile while Nora aimed arrows at the legs of the giants. She was becoming quite a good shot and several of them ran away crying. Pudding hurled himself at the carnivorous jelly and bit mouthfuls off the deadly dessert. I slashed and cut with my sword, but even more nightmares poured into Grimdean House.

The Mara whispered something to the white rabbit, who fixed angry black eyes on me and lunged, roaring, "Chocolate!"

Sammie stared round, her eyes wide. I knew she must be seeing an empty hall. "What's going on, Robyn? I'm scared."

This was quite a big thing for my sarcastic older sister to admit and I would have tried to reassure her if I hadn't been buried under five tonnes of bunny fluff. I elbowed my way out of the rabbit's grip and drew back my sword.

"Chocolate kill!" The rabbit hurled itself at me again, bashing me round the head with its basket.

I reeled and the world spun. Luckily the rabbit stumbled over a crack in the ground, giving me time to recover. Swinging my sword, I hit the creature's stomach, making a long gash which started oozing melted chocolate. I was so stunned that I forgot to dodge and its next blow caught me on the arm, making me drop the sword.

The Mara made a move but I snatched up the weapon again. Sweeping the sword in an arc, I sliced off half the rabbit's whiskers. A deep growl burst from the creature and it yanked open a flap in its stomach and began firing chocolate drops the size of conkers. I shielded my face as the drops hit me like bullets. I caught Sammie's look of bewilderment. I knew I must look unbelievably silly – ducking to avoid the attack of a creature she couldn't see.

After a minute, the chocolate drops ran out. Pudding, who had destroyed the carnivorous jelly, leapt on the rabbit toppling him over before a massive blow from the creature's paw sent him flying. I feinted left and thrust my sword low – a move I'd practised a lot in training. The white rabbit dodged and gripped me by the throat, growling, "Chocolate!"

"I don't have ... any chocolate," I choked out. From the corner of my eye, I saw the Mara smile and edge towards me.

Then Wendy appeared, slicing the air with her sabres. White fluff flew everywhere. The bunny dropped me and Wendy knocked the creature out with one blow.

"Nice one!" I gasped. "Thanks, Wendy!"

"Enough!" The Mara pointed his pale fingers at Pudding and the Chime wolf suddenly crumpled, whining in agony. "Lay down your weapons now or your wolf will die."

"Pudding!" I crouched on the ground beside the wolf.

"You evil monster!" Rufus swung his ultrasonic blade but the Mara took the weapon and snapped it in two.

Pudding whimpered with pain. I looked helplessly at Nora and Aiden, but I could see from their faces that they had no idea what to do.

Sammie looked horrified. "Robyn, call a vet! Can't you see your dog's ill?"

"I know he is, but. . ." I clenched the Sword of Runes tightly. The weapon was important but I would have to give it away. I couldn't let Pudding suffer and the Mara knew that.

The glowing runes on the metal blazed brighter until it seemed as if the whole sword was alight. The nightmares drew back, suddenly afraid. A distant yowl came from inside the walls.

"Give it to me now!" The Mara twisted his fingers and Pudding howled.

Miss Smiting burst through one of the secret doors inside the walls, followed by a stream of monsters escaping from the dungeon. Fire shot from the crike's tail, the gruckle snarled fiercely and the scree sags clicked as they ran. The skitting swooped into the air and the kobolds ran along the ceiling.

The mimicus slid out, squealing, "Give it to ME!"

My shoulders sank. We could never fight them all. Between the nightmares and the monsters, the last tiny crumb of hope was gone. The monsters advanced, crowding round the sword with its blazing runes – drawn to its dark power. I jumped up and held the blade high, hoping to keep it till the very last second.

The fiery runes reflected in the crike's eyes, turning them orange. The gruckle's three eyes changed colour too. The mimicus stuck out ten eyes on stalks and each one transformed. Even the scree sag's creepy white eyes turned the colour of flame.

Nora gasped. "They're under the power of the sword. Quick, Robyn! Tell them what to do!"

I realized she was right. The Sword of Runes had drawn the monsters in and now it had power over them too. "Fight the nightmares!" I commanded, still holding the blade up high. "Destroy every single one of them."

The monsters turned and pounced. The crike blasted fire at the giants. The mimicus rolled over the gnomes, sucking them into its squidgy transparent body. The gruckle jumped at the white rabbit and bit a hole in its basket. Aiden grabbed Sammie's hand and pulled her out of the way while I raced at the Mara with my sword raised.

Caught off guard, the Nightmare Man bared his teeth. I brought the sword down on his head and this time the blade hit home. He staggered. I aimed another blow, striking his shoulder. His pale skin began to glow like fire. The dream leeches on his jacket burst into balls of smoke.

"I will haunt your dreams, Robyn Silver," he snarled. "I will haunt your friends' dreams too and I will turn every night into a storm of terror which you'll beg to escape from."

"The good thing about dreams," I replied, raising my sword again, "is that you can always wake up." I aimed a third blow at his chest. "Anyway I never beg for anything."

Sammie's face was white. "Robyn? Who're you talking to?"

"Stay back!" I warned her as the Mara's skin glowed brighter and brighter. Then, with a fierce pulse of colour, he was gone.

The nightmares began to fade. The crocodile in the bonnet tried to run but became nothing more than a misty shape by the time it reached the street. The gnomes were the last to vanish. Still shaking their table forks at Rufus, they blinked out.

"Thank goodness! I don't think I could take any more." Rufus showed us the fork scratches all over his skin.

"My dears!" Miss Smiting hissed. "What a terrible night – I have been chased by the wraith-gator all over thiss place." She shuddered. "I still get nightmares about how it used to sstalk me round the rainforest. It had three razor-sharp tailss and eyes like lasers." She pulled herself together. "Quickly now! Help me organize these beasts."

The fiery colour was disappearing from the monsters' eyes as the runes on the sword grew dimmer. I knew we didn't have much time before they went back to normal. "Follow us to the dungeon," I commanded them, and they trailed after us quite tamely and returned to their cages. The gruckle growled as I fastened the lock on its pen, but then curled up and fell asleep. The scree sags collapsed into piles of bones. Only the mimicus tried to flee, crying, "I will haunt your dreams!" And it took Aiden and Nora five minutes to squash the creature through the cage door.

"Excellent!" Miss Smiting scanned the dungeon, her piercing green eyes settling on Sammie. My heart lurched. I hadn't realized she'd followed us down here. "Is that your ssister, Robyn? Bring her to Mr Cryptorum's study. We must ensure she rememberss nothing of this night."

In the study, Miss Smiting sat Sammie down in the armchair and gave her a rose quartz crystal, telling her to gaze into the stone. This had worked on people before – the quartz crystal had mind-healing properties, or so Nora said – but I knew Sammie wouldn't like it. I sat on the sofa opposite and watched the normal sarcastic expression creep back on to my sister's face. Rufus was scanning the books on Cryptorum's shelves. Nora and Aiden had gone to the kitchen to make drinks for everyone.

"What am I supposed to do with this pink rock?" Sammie demanded again, turning it over in her hand.

"You gaze into it," Miss Smiting said severely, "and *relax*."

"I've read about this kind of thing. You're trying to hypnotize me, aren't you?" Sammie narrowed her eyes. "I don't believe in that rubbish and anyway I won't be made to do something stupid. I saw a man on the TV hypnotize these people and then he made them dance like chickens."

"If you don't believe in it you shouldn't be afraid of getting hypnotized," I pointed out.

"Well thank you, Miss Freak Brain!" Sammie rolled her eyes. "Now I know what your Bat Club is really about – playing sword fighting with a bunch of little kids and wrecking this place. Wonder what Mum and Dad are going to say about *that*?"

"Robyn, perhapss you and Rufus should go and help Nora and Aiden make the hot chocolate." Miss Smiting shooed us from the room. "I will take care of your ssister, I promise, and help her use the rose quartz crystal until I'm absolutely sure her memory iss wiped clean of the terrible things she saw."

I noticed Sammie rolling her eyes behind us. "But, miss! You'll need help. You don't know her. . ."

"I am quite capable of coping with one stroppy teenager," Miss Smiting said tartly and closed the door on us.

"So what's next?" We heard Sammie say. "Do you have any more crystals? Or maybe you'd like me to eat some herbs and then do some chanting?"

Rufus pulled a face. "Is your sister always like that? She's scary!"

I shook my head. "You have no idea."

20

We Get Surprise Visitors

he whole town was a disaster area for days. People thought it must have been a minor earthquake which cracked the ground open, toppled trees and broke windows. They blamed their bad dreams on the fact the disaster had begun while they were sleeping. That explanation didn't account for the huge yeti footprint in the town square so people took photos of the print until the local paper published a story saying it had been put there as a prank.

Cryptorum arrived home three days after we'd defeated the Mara. He didn't say much about his time in Prague but his face was more deeply lined and his hair greyer than before. The day after he returned, Miss Smiting hired some builders to fix the walls and floor in the Grimdean entrance hall. Nora, Aiden and me took Pudding out into the garden away from all the noise and the dust. Cryptorum had gone upstairs to his study, asking not to be disturbed, and every now and then I saw his silhouette pacing past the window.

"What happened at the Federation headquarters – has he said anything?" I asked the others.

Nora shook her head. "I know he's taken the Sword of Runes to the dungeon because I had to go down there with some grubs and insects for the multi-winged skitting."

A low throbbing sound began in the distance and a helicopter swooped overhead like a bird of prey. The noise grew deafening, drowning out Pudding's barks.

"It's Dray!" I pulled Pudding away from the landing spot. The first time we'd met Dray and the BUTT kids they'd arrived in their helicopter. Dray loved showing off all the expensive things he owned.

The helicopter landed smoothly and I waited for Rufus, Portia and Tristan to leap down with their sleek jackets and ultrasonic blades. Instead, a neat figure with a black briefcase climbed out carefully.

Mr Fettle – the man from the International Federation of Chimes – made a slicing motion with his hand and the pilot turned off the engine. Fettle walked towards us, lay down his briefcase and took out a scroll which unravelled on to the grass. Rufus and Portia and Tristan climbed out after him, followed by Dray. Rufus looked gloomy but Portia was preening as usual.

A wave of anger swept over me at the sight of Mr Fettle and his scroll. The Federation had imprisoned Cryptorum when we needed him most and left us to face the Mara alone. My fingers itched to pull the scroll from his hand and rip it into pieces.

Fettle shot us a disapproving look. "I haven't been able to return as quickly as I hoped. Where is Mr Cryptorum?"

"He's in the house. Shall I fetch him?" Nora offered.

"Never mind, we'll begin without him." Fettle shook the scroll to get out the wrinkles. "There have been some very disturbing developments since I was last here and in the light of these the International Federation of Chimes has a number of new orders which you'll need to adhere to if you wish to continue as a Chime."

He cleared his throat and began to read. "*Order number one: each Chime trainee will undergo a test of their knowledge, fitness and fighting skills every month. If they fail any of these areas they will no longer be a Chime. Order number two: each Chime trainee will hand over every weapon they have ever used for examination by the Federation and if that weapon is deemed to be too powerful it shall be confiscated. . .*"

I exchanged looks with the others. I was pretty sure I knew what this was about. "You want the Sword of Runes, don't you?"

Fettle looked offended at being interrupted. "Young lady, I don't remember your name but—"

"I'm Robyn Silver," I said. "I struck the Mara with the Sword of Runes and destroyed him – no thanks to you or anyone else at the Federation." I turned to Dray. "And no thanks to you either! You knew the sword was important and you kept that a secret because you wanted it for yourself. Your Wendy robot was more help than you."

"Silence, you insolent girl!" Dray seethed but Fettle raised a hand to quiet him.

"I see you think yourself very brave, being cheeky in this way. No doubt you got lucky with this sword and struck the monster by accident."

The Federation man rolled the scroll back up. "Fetch the weapon and I'll see whether there is *actually* anything out-of-the-ordinary about it."

Blood was humming in my ears. *Struck the monster by accident!* "No, I'm not giving the sword to you."

Fettle's face darkened. "Fetch it now – any more defiance and you will no longer be allowed to train as a Chime."

I folded my arms. "How are you going to stop me fighting monsters? You can visit and read out your silly orders a billion times but it won't make any difference to what happens when you're not here."

"Robyn. . ." Nora hissed.

"Well it's true!" I said. "And by the way I'm not doing any of your tests either."

Dray advanced on me, pointing his cane at my face. "Now listen, Robyn Silver—"

"Get away from her, Dominic, or you and I will come to blows." Cryptorum blocked the cane easily with the Sword of Runes.

"Helmfist's Sword!" Fettle stared at the runes on the blade.

"I don't want to fight with you, Erasmus," Dray said. "And I don't know what the children told you, but I had no idea your old sword was an artefact of vital importance. I discovered the last piece of information the night the Mara attacked but by then it was impossible to get hold of you."

"Yeah, I bet." Cryptorum managed a grim smile. "I was stuck in a Federation jail accused of obstructing Chime business. They took weeks to decide they were mistaken and let me go, but perhaps you didn't hear about that?"

"Dreadful!" Dray shook his head. "But the sword! Can you really be naïve enough to expect everything to be fine if you keep the weapon here? We know it draws in monsters – goodness knows how it possesses such power. . ."

Rufus spoke up. "It was made by an ogre called Helmfist – he planned to bring an army of monsters against the Chimes. He added his own blood when he melted down the metal to make the sword. I found it all out from a book in our library."

"I must have missed that one," Nora murmured.

Dray tried to cover his surprise. "Well done, Rufus. All the more reason to send it to headquarters, Erasmus. The sword is cursed."

Cryptorum was silent for a moment. "I don't think I will. I don't trust the Federation any more than I trust you, Dominic. Robyn, Aiden, Nora, come inside now and bring that Chime wolf with you." He turned his back on the visitors. "See yourselves out, gentlemen, and if you come here again without an invitation I shall set my bats on you."

Dray looked furious. "Suit yourself! Rufus, Portia, Tristan – back to the helicopter. I'm finished with trying to help people who don't deserve it."

Portia and Tristan climbed back on board but Rufus hung back. "Mr Cryptorum?" he called. "Could I ask you something?"

"Rufus!" Dray said sharply.

Cryptorum swung round. "What is it, young man?"

"I'd like to ... I mean, would you let me learn at Grimdean House and become one of your trainees?" Rufus hurried on, ignoring Portia's shout of protest. "I fought here the night the Mara came and ... well I'd like to fight here again, if you see what I mean."

Cryptorum did one of his big smiles like the sun coming out after a rainstorm. "That's a strange turn!" He looked at me, Nora and Aiden. "Well? Do you have any objections?"

"Not from me," Aiden replied.

"I think it's great!" Nora said.

Cryptorum glanced at me and lifted one eyebrow. I grinned and said, "Hey, Rufus, I guess there's some hope for you after all!"

"Just to be clear, Cryptorum," Fettle said coldly. "If you refuse to give me Helmfist's Sword and to let me test your trainees, you'll be thrown out of the International Federation of Chimes. Seeking out monsters to fight will be forbidden and if you do so anyway you will be punished. There will be no warnings and no excuses. Your trainees will be sent a new Federation-approved instructor. They will be in charge of these children and you will be punished if you interfere."

"What? You can't send another instructor here!" I cried. "We don't want anyone else training us."

"It's all right, Robyn." Cryptorum fixed Fettle with a glare. "The Federation has insulted me, threatened me and locked me up already. You say there's more to come – well I say bring it on!" With a swing of the sword, he marched towards the house.

Fettle's face was expressionless as he clicked his briefcase shut and returned to the helicopter.

"Your sword and watch please, Rufus," Dray said icily, and Rufus put the watch and ultrasonic blade into his outstretched hand. "Don't think you can ever come back to us. I just hope you don't come to regret your choice."

"Don't worry – he won't," Aiden said.

Rufus stood with us as we watched Dray's helicopter zoom into the cloudy sky.

I went to find Cryptorum later after we'd shown Rufus the important stuff – where the cookies were kept and how to spook people by peering through the eyes of the paintings from inside the secret passage in the walls.

Cryptorum was in the dungeon, looping long chains around a wooden chest and fastening it with a padlock. The crike was snoring softly and the scree sag was rattling the bars of its cage.

"Is the Sword of Runes in there?" I nodded to the chest.

"No, Robyn I'm just locking the chest with lots of chains for fun!" he grumbled. "Yes of course the sword is in there."

"It was weird, the way the sword commanded the monsters – almost as if it brainwashed them for a while," I said. "If I could get the sword to do that all the time it would be pretty handy. I could command the monsters to be tame and—"

"You'd be more likely to cause a disaster." Cryptorum closed the padlock firmly. "That sword is unpredictable. It was made by a monster for use against the Chimes and that means any Chime that tries to use it is playing with fire. If I'd known what it was I would have locked it away years ago or found a way to destroy it."

I sighed. I knew he was right but I couldn't help thinking it was a waste of a good sword.

"There are consequences from all this," Cryptorum continued. "Only the most powerful warriors can wield the Sword of Runes, but you managed it and that means the Federation now knows exactly how strong you are. That's why they're sending a new teacher here – to keep an eye on you."

"Oh!" My heart sank.

Cryptorum checked the padlock and dusted off his hands. "So I suppose we'd better get some proper training done before they arrive. But first I need to get these monsters back to the wild – those that are safe to release anyway."

The crike opened one eye and yawned. I remembered how the monsters fought the nightmares for us the night the Mara came. "I'd like to help free them, if that's all right."

"Free them! Free them!" echoed the mimicus, as if it knew exactly what we were saying.

Cryptorum looked at me under his eyebrows. "You kids can do it together. After all, you defeated the Nightmare Man. I suppose it's about time I let you take more responsibility."

21

I Make a Truce With My Sister

hen I got back home Annie and Josh were fighting a major battle over a small rubber lizard.

"It's mine!" Annie shouted. "I have two of them and you've taken one already! This is the only one I have left."

Josh yanked it out of her hand.

"That's enough!" Mum snapped. "Annie, you've probably lost the other one. It's probably somewhere in your room – under the bed maybe."

"I was playing with them in here." Annie's face was bright pink.

"Well, look around! There are plenty of places for toys to get lost here too." Mum noticed me in the doorway. "Come and help Robyn. You too, Sammie."

Sammie made an irritated noise in her throat and switched off the TV. Mum crouched on the floor, sweeping her hand under the sofa. Then she checked behind the sofa cushions. "Whose is this?" She held up my torchblade. "What does this extra button do?" I held my breath as her finger hovered over the button which made the sword appear.

"It's mine!" Sammie snatched it out of her hand. "That button's just a different light setting. Thanks, I'll put it away."

I pretended to search for a minute so as not to look suspicious, then I followed Sammie upstairs. I couldn't believe I'd left the torchblade on the sofa. It must have slipped out of my pocket when I was sitting down. Knocking on my sister's bedroom door, I went inside.

Sammie was sitting on her bed reading a book. "What do you want dork brain?"

"I want my torch back. Why did you take it?" I'd assumed this was a standard Sammie wind-up but there was no smirk on her face.

She chewed her lip, then pulled the torchblade out of a cupboard. "Here you go then. I guess you might need it." I took it and turned to go. "By the way, you'd better be careful at that Grimdean Bat

Club. *I* don't care if you lose a couple of limbs but Mum and Dad wouldn't like it."

"What do you mean?"

"Nothing. It's just that I know what a disaster area you are."

I looked at her for a minute. Did she remember something from the night the Mara came? The rose quartz crystal should have cleaned away those bad memories but maybe Sammie's mind clung to things like a crab with strong pincers. It wouldn't surprise me. "I guess you wonder what we really do at Bat Club," I managed.

"Not really." She went back to her book, turning the page.

My heart was racing now. If she remembered something. . . "Have you ever seen a pink-coloured crystal? Miss Smiting has one and she may have shown it to you."

Sammie looked up and winked. "What crystal?"

I swallowed. "Look whatever you think you know. . ."

"Your secrets are safe with me, dork brain, as long as you don't mess up my stuff. Now go away – you're spreading younger sister germs." I turned to the door. "And Robyn? Seriously, don't get yourself killed."

"I'll try not to." I stuck the torchblade in my pocket and went downstairs. Sammie knew about the Chime world. That meant we were probably all doomed!

"Don't you think you should take the rose quartz home and try to wipe her memories again?" Aiden said, when I told them all about Sammie. "She could completely blow our cover! Everyone in Wendleton would know what we do."

"They'd never believe her – not without evidence," Nora said thoughtfully, "and it's not as if they can see the monsters."

We were standing together in the middle of Blagdurn Heath the next day – just me, Aiden, Nora and Rufus. Miss Smiting, who had driven us up here, was waiting in the van. The heath was blanketed in mist, softening the outlines of the muddy ditches and stubby trees. There was a row of cages at our feet. We'd come here to free some of the monsters from the dungeon – those that wouldn't be a danger if they were living in the middle of nowhere. Cryptorum wasn't with us. He'd taken the beasts like the crike that needed a hot climate on a long road trip south.

"I don't think she'll tell everyone," I said. "She's

more likely to use what she knows to get what she wants from me."

"That's the sort of thing my older brother does," Rufus agreed.

"Maybe it'll be a good thing," Nora said brightly. "It could bring you closer together."

I smiled. Nora always had a rosy view of what having brothers and sisters was like, maybe because she didn't have any of her own. But she was right in a way – Sammie had been pretty nice about things earlier and she'd stopped Mum from accidentally pressing the torchblade sword button.

Aiden knelt by the row of cages. "OK, who's going first?"

"Whooo's going first?" cried the mimicus, slithering up and down its cage.

Aiden unfastened the cage and the mimicus slid out, gaining speed as it headed for the nearest patch of swamp. I undid the jooper's pen and it bounded away as if delighted to be free.

"It's nice to see them out of that dungeon. I guess we owe them something after that fight with the Mara," I said.

"Yes, but is it worth being prickled to death," Rufus yelped, as the kobold he'd just released jumped on him, spines bristling. "Can we go back now and have some more hot chocolate?"

I pulled the kobold off him and pushed it towards a clump of bushes. "We don't have time to mess around! We need to get lots of training done so we can face the next big monster."

"And we need to finish reading the books in Cryptorum's study," Nora added. "I found some great new ones on wraiths and ghouls."

"And I have lots more ideas for new gadgets," Aiden said.

"Jeez! Don't you ever have a rest?" Rufus rolled his eyes.

I grinned and slapped him on the back. "Don't worry, you'll get used to it. You're a Grimdean Chime now." I leaned down to open the last cage.

The multi-winged skitting hopped out, spread its wings and soared towards the tangled wood on the far side of the heath. There'd been a time when I thought seeing monsters was a curse – that I'd been unlucky to be born at midnight. Now I was glad that I could see them. I would always be able to protect the people that couldn't.

We gathered the empty cages and headed back along the muddy path. Miss Smiting revved the engine when she saw us coming. The setting sun glowed cheerfully behind the trees, as if the battles of yesterday were nothing more than a bad dream.

DREAM LEECH

DREAM LEECH

These black bugs with shiny
wings may be small, but beware!
They will give you nasty
nightmares before bursting
into a puff of grey smoke.

CRIKE

CRIKE

Looks like a dragon crossed with a lion — and has a fiery temper to match. When those red spikes round its neck bristle, there's only one thing to do: RUN!

HELL WURM

HELL WURM

A colossal, vicious creature with
a rubbery body that oozes slime.
Don't ask it to smile nicely
for the camera — its rows
of teeth are razor-sharp.

JOOPER

JOOPER

A monster always found jumping
up and down like a particularly
bizarre pogo stick – stay out
of the way of those fangs!

GRUCKLE

GRUCKLE

This huge dog with three eyes
definitely isn't in the mood for
rolling over and having its tummy
tickled... beware, its bark is
equally as bad as its bite.

MIMICUS

MIMICUS

Is there an echo in here? This jelly-like, squelching creature will repeat everything you say — making it as annoying as it is odd-looking!

MULTI-WINGED
SKITTING

MULTI-WINGED SKITTING

You may think a flock of budgies is flying towards you, but look closer... it's an enormous winged creature with a room-rattling squawk and dangerous talons.

THE MARA

THE MARA

You really don't want to meet
this monster on a dark night...
ghost-white skin, blank eyes and
a cavernous mouth full of teeth as
sharp as a shark's... the stuff of
your very worst nightmare.

TROFFLEGURT

TROFFLEGURT

The handyman of the monster world – this small, stubby, constantly burbling creature is covered in grey hair and has a dozen fingers on each hand, all the better for fixing any malfunctioning equipment.

Don't miss Robyn's
first amazing adventure!

Robyn Silver

THE
MIDNIGHT
CHIMES

PAULA HARRISON